'Waste no more time arguing about what a good man should be. Be one.'

Marcus Aurelius

Emperor of Rome 121-180 AD

One

The shriek startled Danny from his daydream. He turned around as a torrent of abuse followed it, not the sort of thing you expect to hear from a pretty, blonde woman outside the local supermarket on a sunny Saturday afternoon in late September. Later on, maybe, when night fell, and a few drinks had loosened some tongues, but not at this time of the day.

As others turned to see what was going on, Danny saw the light blue, hooded top, blue jeans and dirty white trainers of someone running towards him. He also saw the bright red handbag with gold trim clutched under the thief's arm. *Someone should have told him it doesn't match his outfit.*

'Stop him, the little shit! He's got my bag!' shouted the pretty woman. Without a second thought, Danny stuck his foot out, tripping the lanky thief mid-stride.

He tumbled along the pavement like a sack of potatoes falling off a tractor on a bumpy country lane. He came to a grinding halt as he collided with an old lady shuffling along with a tartan shopping trolley. She went down like a pin in a bowling alley, and there was a sickening crack and a groan as she hit the pavement. Shoppers close by rushed to help.

Danny discarded his shopping and marched over to the dark-haired figure sprawled face up on the pavement. He dropped down knees first, concentrating all his weight onto the thief's chest, knocking the wind out of him and probably cracking a rib in the process. *It was no more than the little shit deserved. Anyone stealing handbags and knocking over little old ladies should be treated with nothing less than contempt.*

A fist was thrown at Danny's head, but he brushed it aside. He then proceeded to pummel the face beneath him. He took his time, ensuring maximum damage, the gold ring on the third finger of his left hand drawing blood.

The owner of the stolen handbag ran over and stood next to them. It was clear to her that the thief couldn't defend himself against Danny's onslaught. He looked close to unconsciousness.

'Danny, stop!' she shouted, grabbing hold of his arm midswing.

He was snarling as he turned towards her, eyes wide with rage. She'd seen that look before but had hoped – after last time – she'd never see it again. 'That's enough,' she said calmly, maintaining eye contact and keeping a tight hold on his arm. He stared at her for a moment and turned back to the thief, now covered in blood and moaning. Danny's shoulders slumped, and his expression softened as the tension in his muscles began to ease.

A small crowd had gathered around them. 'Jeez, that's a bit over the top,' someone said on seeing the bloodied face of the thief.

'He looks like he needs help,' someone else said.

Danny got to his feet and turned to face the crowd, shaking his head in disbelief.

'This tosser just stole my wife's purse and knocked that woman over,' he said, pointing at the old lady whimpering in pain on the pavement. 'Why do you want to help him? He's scum and deserves everything he gets.' The crowd retreated like a flock of sheep being herded by a snarling dog. No one wanted to get in the way of his anger or his bloodied fists.

'He wouldn't have knocked her over if you hadn't tripped him up,' said a middle-aged woman with folded arms and a cigarette hanging from her unpainted lips.

The crowd murmured and nodded in agreement. 'Call an ambulance,' said the smoker.

'Call the bizzies,' said the woman next to her.

Jackie picked up her favourite red handbag from where the thief had dropped it and grabbed hold of Danny. The police would take one look at the 6' tall, stocky guy with bloodied fists and decide that the skinny boy covered in blood had been the innocent victim of an assault. They could do without the police and their foregone conclusions.

A newcomer joined the crowd. 'Is that Ryan Thomson?' he asked. 'Shit, what happened to his face?'

Jackie noticed a few people step forward with something other than fear in their eyes. 'Get the shopping Danny and let's go.'

'We haven't done anything wrong,' he said defiantly, oblivious to the change in mood around them. 'Why are we running away?'

She was becoming impatient but forced herself to stay calm. Now was not the time to stand and argue. 'Let's go,' she said through gritted teeth, pushing him through the crowd.

Two

By the time they got back to the safety of their high-rise flat, Mr Angry had disappeared. Danny was going through a period of clarity quickly followed by remorse as he reflected on the consequences of his actions. Something unpleasant usually happened when his temper got the better of him. Jackie had often asked him what was going on in his head when he flared up like that. She got the standard reply from her apologetic husband.

'It just happens. It's like a switch that turns on a light without warning. I have no control over it.'

Even after all their years together, she still found it hard to understand. They put the shopping away in awkward silence, and Danny waited for the inevitable inquest into what had happened.

The sun was streaming into the lounge through the open balcony door, reflecting off Jackie's long, blonde hair as she sat next to him on the worn, grey sofa. He rubbed his finger across the scar over his right eyebrow – an unwanted gift from his sister when he was 18. Sue had thrown a can of beer at him during an argument at his birthday party, and it had cut him just above his eye. It needed three stitches, and after it healed, he realised that he subconsciously rubbed it when he was nervous, as he did now. The sofa creaked as they settled in for their chat. It reminded him of the sofa in the waiting room next to the school headmaster's office that had also creaked when he sat on it. So long ago, he thought, but here I am again waiting to be told off. Jackie's voice broke into his memories.

'Danny, this can't go on. You're going to kill someone if you can't control yourself. You said you'd got a handle on it, but that's not how it looks to me, or anyone else for that matter. Do you have any idea how much you frighten me when you're like that? What you did to that lad today could have left him disfigured. You could have gone to jail. You've got to promise me that you'll get counselling.'

He began to protest, but she cut him off.

'No, no more excuses! I'm not going to be around forever; who's going to keep you out of trouble if I'm not here? It doesn't matter what it costs; you need it. If you like, I'll go with you, and we'll try and sort it out together. Please, Danny, before you do something we can't fix. Promise me you'll go.'

He looked into her emerald-green eyes, kissed her gently and promised.

Three

The man getting into the passenger seat of the dark blue Range Rover was wearing a fitted, grey suit with a white, open-necked shirt that revealed an exquisite gold chain. It had been given to him by his mother. He thought the world of her, but that didn't make him a nice guy. On the contrary, he could be ruthless.

***

Terry Lynch remembered being a happy-go-lucky teenager when his dad passed away. Overnight he became the man of the house. Life had been hard, but it had shaped the person he'd become. He never dreamt he would grow up to be the man he was today because there wasn't time to dream back then, but now his achievements were there for everyone to see.

The days he lived with his mother and brother in their grotty two-up two-down terraced house on Norfolk Street were a distant memory, but never too distant – it wasn't good to take things for granted. After a few years when the money started rolling in, he bought his mum a detached bungalow in Higher Runcorn, just off Greenway Road. He could have bought her a place anywhere, but she chose to stay where she'd grown up and raised her family.

She loved to walk to the high street, do her shopping and have a natter with her mates. That had been her daily routine for as long as he could remember. Family and friends were everything to her.

She had used some of her savings to buy him the gold chain he wore around his neck as a thank you for her new home. It meant a lot to him.

To say he was unhappy when he found out that some tosser had knocked his mum over outside the supermarket was an understatement. It didn't matter that it was an accident. What did matter was that she was in hospital with a broken hip.

The person who caused this pain and suffering had been attempting to steal a woman's handbag. A knight in shining armour apparently stepped in and gave the thief a good hiding. As far as Terry was concerned, the only casualty was his mum.

He made a few phone calls to the right people with the unspoken promise of favours in return for information, and it wasn't long before he was given the name of the tosser.

The search for Ryan Thomson began.

***

Lance Corporal Charlie Edwards had been a teenager when he joined the army. After breaking his arm in an unlucky accident, he found himself confined to light duties for six weeks. While waiting for his arm to heal, it struck him how much of his everyday life he took for granted. It was hard to get dressed with one arm in a cast, and taking a piss was a nightmare. With nothing to do, he began to drink heavily.

One time, after a few too many afternoon beers, he complained to the canteen cook about the tasteless army food he served up. The sympathetic chef produced a large bag of chilli peppers.

'Charlie, this is what we need! A bit of spice!' he said.

The cook explained the different colours and heat ratings to the small group that had gathered round and bit into a small red chilli. Grinning he held it out for someone else to try. A couple of squaddies took a bite of another small red one and immediately downed copious amounts of water to douse the fire raging in their mouths. Always up for a challenge, Charlie popped a whole one in his mouth. Everyone cheered when he punched the air in triumph but his smile faded as the chilli bomb took effect. He turned white and threw up everywhere.

From then on, his nickname was Chilli.

He'd had been in the Army for five years and had loved every minute of it. His time there had prepared him for a bright future in the outside world.

Soldiers do as they're told, and as one of Terry Lynch's men, he was happy to follow orders. A guilty conscience was not something he thought about.

Four

Toward the end of his time at school, the careers advisor put Terry in touch with someone at the local factory who gave him a job on the tools, fixing things. It wasn't a formal training apprenticeship, more of a 'go and find out what's wrong and sort it' kind of job. He didn't mind. He enjoyed being out of the classroom, earning a living and looking after his mum. The money was okay, and he was good with his hands. He was a quick learner and trained to become one of the factory firefighters and a first aider.

He got on with most people at the factory but eventually crossed paths with the workplace bully, Mike Stevens, who took an instant dislike to him. Despite Terry's best efforts to avoid him, their paths eventually crossed. He was on his way to look at a faulty door handle in the offices when they passed in the corridor. Mike punched Terry in the face. It hadn't been a particularly hard punch, but the shock of it dropped Terry to one knee.

He felt anger at being attacked for no apparent reason and shame at being caught off-guard. The humiliation was more upsetting than the punch. He knew he would remember that feeling for the rest of his life. Mike walked on as if nothing had happened. Terry decided he couldn't leave it at that. He seldom looked for a fight, but he had mucked about with his brother and enjoyed a tussle with him. They'd had fights in the garden from a young age, which Terry always won, but this was different. The attack was unprovoked, and the interaction was not mutual. He also didn't like the idea of losing.

'Hey,' he shouted.

Mike turned around with a look of surprise as Terry walked towards him.

His victims didn't usually come back for more.

'What do you want scrote?'

Terry saw a flicker of uncertainty in Mike's eyes. He' d seen a similar look when he stood over his brother at the end of their fights. *Was he scared?*

'I'm going to punch you in the face. The same as you punched me, but harder,' Terry said. 'At least I'll have a reason to do it. You hit me for no reason. Just because you don't like me doesn't mean you have the right to hit me.'

'You're full of shit,' Mike said. 'Piss off before I really hurt you.'

'Not before I give you this.'

As Terry stepped forward on his left leg, he dropped his right arm and made a fist. Mike had seen what was coming and moved to his right. Terry anticipated this and planted a left handed punch on Mike's chin. His right hand would have been more powerful, but Mike's momentum as he moved toward him did the trick. Moving his right hand had been a feint, a distraction, something he'd learnt fighting his brother, and it had worked. Mike staggered back a couple of feet but didn't go down.

Terry remembered when the science teacher at school had explained force, energy and momentum. Science was not his favourite subject, but when Mr Brophy had used the mechanics of a punch as an example, he had Terry's full attention.

'A good punch,' he'd said, 'is the result of the entire body working together. When a punch connects, a lot of energy is released. It starts in the feet, working through the legs, into the torso, over the shoulders and eventually explodes out of the fist. The impact of this energy on the human head can be devastating, causing the brain to slam against the inside of the skull, creating trauma. Are you with me so far?' he'd asked the class.

All the boys nodded enthusiastically.

'This can happen many times until the energy from the blow reverberates like an echo in a valley. Overwhelmed by the trauma, the brain shuts down, rendering a person unconscious. In other words, it would knock you out.'

Terry stood staring at Mike, prepared for whatever came next..

Wiping the blood from his lip, Mike said, 'I'll give you that one. I probably deserved it.'

That was the first time anyone other than his brother had been on the receiving end of Terry's idea of fair play.

Five

Gary, Terry's brother, was also a teenager when their dad died. He went off the rails without his dad to keep him in check and started hanging around with the wrong crowd. As he got to know them, he decided that what they offered was better than anything he had at home.

He didn't go to school much after that and often got into fights. It wasn't long before he started smoking weed and paying for it with stolen money. He and a couple of his new mates thought it would be a good idea to steal from their dealer. *It's better than paying for it, right!*

The dealer wasn't much older than them and didn't seem to have anyone looking out for him, so one day, after picking up their weed, they beat him badly and left him for dead. Gary hadn't signed up to kill anyone and ran away. He didn't want to, but in the end he went to Terry and pleaded with him to go and help the dealer. It turned out to be a wise decision. Terry managed to revive him and get him to hospital.

They later found out that the dealer didn't need protection because his father was a gangland boss in Liverpool. If Gary and his mates had taken the time to ask around, they would have known that. Not long after, Gary's two mates were found badly beaten at the docks in Liverpool. They suffered life-changing injuries.

Two weeks later, when Gary thought it was safe to come out of hiding and visit his mum, two men tried to take him outside her house. Terry intervened and sent them away with their tails between their legs. Frank Murphy, the gangland boss, eventually caught up with Gary. 'You mess with the Murphy family, you get hurt. You hear me!'

Gary pleaded with him. 'I never wanted that to happen, Mr Murphy. I didn't know they would do that. My brother's the one who took Sean to hospital. He saved his life, please—'

'That was your brother? I want to speak to him!'

Terry wasn't happy about going to meet a gang boss but gave in after Gary told him he was as good as dead if he didn't. Murphy was grateful to Terry for saving his sons life, but he wouldn't let Gary off the hook.

'Terry, your brother owes me big time. I want payment for the five kilo's of weed him and his mates stole from my son. Ten grand should cover it. When can I expect payment?'

'I don't have that kind of money, Mr Murphy. I work in a factory, and I look after my mum and brother. Gary is his own man.'

Frank stared at him for a few seconds, appraising the young man standing proudly in front of him.

'This is how I see things, Terry. Either your brother pays me what he owes, or I take one of his eyes. Alternatively, you come and work for me and pay off your brothers debt.'

He waited patiently for Terry to realise that he had no choice.

Terry gave his brother a look of irritation and turned to Murphy.

'I suppose I'll have to work for you or try and explain to my mum why her wayward son only has one eye.'

A month later, Terry was working for Frank Murphy in Liverpool.

'You owe me, Gary,' Terry said. 'I've had to give up my job and move away to save your arse. You're going to have to step up, get a job and look after mum while I'm paying off your debts and cleaning up your mess.'

'No chance, I'm not takin' orders from you. You're not my boss!' Gary said.

Overcome with anger, Terry punched him in the face and stood over him as he fell.

'Doing what you like is what got you and me into this mess. Think about someone else for a change and do the right thing. If you don't, so help me, I'll tell Frank I won't work for him anymore.'

Gary was horrified. 'But that means—'

'Yes. We both know what that means, and don't think I won't do it if you step out of line again.'

Gary wiped his mouth and got up.

'Okay,' he said, barely able to conceal how angry he was that his brother had control over his life.

Working for Murphy, Terry had unknowingly found an outlet for the pent up anger he felt at his brother's failures and the loss of his father. He repaid the debt he owed for Gary's protection, and when Frank Murphy died unexpectedly some years later, everyone looked to Terry to take his place. Franks son did not have what it took to run the business, and it was too late for Terry to return to the life he had before – the things he'd done in the name of Frank Murphy over the years couldn't be left behind.

Six

Chilli used to enjoy his job, but not anymore. He'd been an executive protection agent for Terry Lynch – the top dog in Liverpool for the last twenty years. It paid well, and getting his hands dirty was in the job description. He was well thought of by his boss and respected by the other gangs in the city. His good looks and his dick, however, were his undoing.

Sophie Lynch was beautiful, a well-proportioned blonde bombshell, and she knew it. She was attracted to well-built men and was the reason Chilli had been forced to leave Liverpool.

Sophie flirted with the men who worked for Terry, but she went overboard when Chilli was around. 'Do I look good in this dress?' she'd ask, posing and strutting in front of him, making sure he got a good eyeful of her long legs and a peek at her surgically altered boobs. It was an odds-on certainty they would sleep together. Chilli didn't care that she was married to Terry's brother, nor did he mind that she had a reputation for sleeping around. If Gary couldn't control his wife, that was his problem.

They ended up together on the living room floor when Gary was supposed to be away on business. He'd come home earlier than expected and caught them at it. Terry had warned Chilli not to get involved with her, but it went in one ear and out the other. Before Gary could kill Chilli, Terry moved him to Runcorn to take care of his interests there. That was two years ago.

Chilli didn't like the small-minded people in the town where Terry had grown up. He wanted to be back in Liverpool and did whatever he could to make that happen. Today, however, wasn't going to be as tedious as every other day. Chilli had phoned his boss to let him know he'd found the druggie who put his mum in hospital. They were going to meet at the unit and even the score.

Seven

It was a bright and sunny Sunday morning as Terry sat outside the industrial unit playing with the gold ring on the little finger of his left hand. The unit was a good place for a quiet chat. He'd used it back in the day to store stolen goods until he could move them on when the heat had died down. Chilli used it to do the same sort of thing – stashing illegal contraband to sell on when the time was right. There were a couple of motorbikes, a quad bike, TVs, laptops, lawnmowers, and even a chainsaw that Chilli had bought for £20 from a disgruntled council worker after he'd been sacked for stealing it.

There was an office desk in one corner and a couple of mismatched wooden chairs that you might see in a trendy cafe on the high street. A metal shutter had a door cut into it that served as the entrance, and at the back, the fire exit had a chain wrapped around the push bar to stave off uninvited guests. It was run-down and visits were by invitation only. No one was going to bother them.

It wasn't long before he heard a car outside, and Chilli came in dragging the druggie thief Ryan Thomson behind him. Terry guessed that Ryan was a little older than his 22 year old son, Jason. Unlike Jason, this kid had not had an easy life. His greasy black hair needed cutting, and a hot shower would do wonders for him. His clothes were dirty and smelt like they'd been hanging on a 'last chance' clothes rail in a charity shop. They sat him down and tied him to one of the wooden chairs next to the desk.

Terry slowly walked around the desk until he stood behind Ryan.

'You little bastard!' Terrys spittle hit the back of Ryan's head. Ryan tried to turn but only succeeded in cricking his neck. Terry moved around to look him in the eye.

'My mum was in hospital last night because of you!'

Ryan looked confused. 'What you sayin'? I haven't put anyone in the hospital. Is that what this is about? Honestly, mate, you've got the wrong guy.'

Terry slapped him across the face, then leant in close enough to see his reflection in the frightened lamb's eyes in front of him.

'I'm not your mate, arsehole. My name is Terry Lynch. You will call me Mr Lynch. Do you understand?'

Ryan nodded frantically, trying to ignore his stinging cheek.

'If you forget everything else about today,' Terry said, 'never forget that!'

Terry walked away and took a few seconds to calm himself. He couldn't let his temper get the better of him. Killing the kid wouldn't achieve anything and might cause him some hassle. He took a deep breath and turned to face Ryan.

'Do you remember stealing a woman's handbag outside the supermarket on the high street yesterday?'

Ryan furrowed his brow. *Wish I hadn't tried nickin' that bag. All that effort for two black eyes and a face full of scratches. At least she stopped that maniac before he broke my nose. Anyway, what's it got to do with this numpty? Nuffin!*

He looked up and smiled, sure of himself. 'Yeh, I did nick a bag from a woman on the high street yesterday, but it wasn't your mum Mr Lynch. No disrespect, but she wasn't old enough.'

'You knocked an old lady over as you cartwheeled along the pavement. Remember?' He paused for effect and shouted 'That was my mum!'

The words hit Ryan like a car crash. He did remember connecting with someone as he fell, but he'd been too busy with his aerial acrobatics to worry about who he'd knocked over. *Shit.*

Terry watched as the colour drained from Ryan's face.

'You broke my mum's hip, you tosser. Now I am going to break your arm.'

Eight

Danny and Jackie got together at secondary school and hadn't been apart since. As soon as they left school and started working, they saved every penny for a deposit they could use to rent a home for themselves. After a couple of years, they eventually found a flat they could afford in the Queen Street block near the town centre. Once that was sorted, it wasn't long before they got married. The service was held at All Saints church around the corner from the flats, and the reception was at the War Memorial Hall off Greenway Road. Everyone agreed that their wedding had been a fantastic day.

Their ninth floor flat had been their home for over 20 years. It was the only block of flats for miles, and it stood like a monolith across the landscape. It was built in the sixties and desperately needed modernising. A lick of paint to the exterior every decade or so had not been enough to stop the rot. Like Danny and Jackie, most residents had lived there for years, enjoying the enviable views from their balconies.

The river Mersey meandered past the back of the flats from the North Sea, through Liverpool and into Warrington. The Silver Jubilee Bridge that crossed the river to the left of them was an unashamed copy of the Sydney Harbour Bridge and was declared open by the Queen in July 1961. Every November, it played host to an impressive fireworks display that people travelled miles to see. Jackie and Danny always made it a special night and danced on the balcony with the fireworks exploding in the sky above them.

On the other side of the river surrounded by trees, stood St Mary's Church. The bell ringers at St Mary's and All Saints churches would practise their campanology skills on Thursday evenings. Sometimes it sounded like a choir of heavenly angels. Sometimes it sounded like a parliament of unruly magpies, but the practice paid off, and the bells rang out in harmony every Sunday morning, echoing through the air, calling the faithful to their knees.

The flat itself was clean, bright and homely. Like everyone who lived on this side of the block, they made the most of the view. The balcony was only big enough for a small table and two foldaway chairs. It had a metal railing at about waist height and a piece of clear, toughened glass below it. Danny and Jackie spent a lot of time there, watching sunsets, drinking wine and telling stories.

After trying for a few years to have kids, they found out they could not conceive. They couldn't afford the recommended IVF treatment, so they just got on with their lives together.

Danny loved Jackie more than anything he could put into words. It was a standing joke at parties and family occasions that Danny always grabbed hold of her after a few too many drinks and loudly proclaimed his feelings for her.

'I love you to the moon and back,' he'd shout at the top of his voice.

Everyone smiled and asked him when he was going to grow up.

He'd laugh and reply, 'There's nothing wrong with being young at heart.'

Nine

Six months ago, all the residents in the block received a letter from the council saying that TL Holdings Ltd, a housing company in Liverpool, was purchasing the block

Once the new owners took over, everything started to change – and not in a good way. The rent increased gradually, which most residents guessed would happen as the company had promised to update the building and repair their flats. The refurbishment was extremely slow. Urgent repairs were delayed and getting hold of anyone to discuss anything was almost impossible.

A help line had been set-up to answer any queries, but when anyone phoned the office an answering machine kicked in requesting callers to leave a message and expect a call-back. Danny left voicemails about a few issues in their flat, including the corroded handrail on the balcony, but no one called back. Eventually, he managed to speak to a young girl he presumed had forgotten to turn on the answering machine that day. She apologised for the delay in getting back to him and told Danny she would put him on the contractor's repairs list.

'Can you give me an idea of the timescale?' he asked her.

'I can't give you a date at the moment,' she said. 'There's a backlog of jobs to sort out.'

'How far down the list am I?'

'About 18 months,' she said.

Danny couldn't believe it.

The four tenants on the tenth floor were 'asked' to leave because the new owners wanted to convert their flats into a penthouse suite. They all refused to go, so a representative was sent round to persuade them to see things from a different point of view. Strong-arm tactics and threats had the desired effect on three of the tenants.

One night, Danny heard shouting and banging from the last occupied flat and went upstairs. The door was open, and Chris, the tenant, was sitting slumped on the floor with his face in his hands. Blood seeped through his fingers and dripped onto the carpet. A gorilla-sized man stood over him.

'You made it difficult. I warned you not to.'

Danny stood at the door. 'Hey, what are you doing?'

The gorilla glared at him. 'What's it to you?'

'I live downstairs. Go now, or I'll call the police.'

Danny took his phone out of his pocket and pressed the keypad. The gorilla slowly walked towards the door, casually catching Danny in the face with his elbow as he passed.

'You got in the way,' he said matter-of-factly.

Danny swayed and dropped to his knees on the carpet next to Chris.

Ten

A local news reporter had once tried to expose Terry Lynch and his underhand ways.

'Terry Lynch is the perfect example of a cat that always lands on its feet. No matter how much trouble he gets into, he always comes out of it with a smile on his face. He is the instigator of most of the criminal activities in the area but has never been held accountable.'

Terry loved talking to the press outside the courts. 'If I'm not proven guilty in a court of law, then I'm innocent. Simple as that. And if anyone says otherwise, I'll sue them for slander' was his standard reply when interviewed after yet another 'not guilty' verdict.

It helped that the network of people he could call on included magistrates, solicitors, police, just about anyone who would turn a blind eye for a little extra cash. His court appearances were just the tip of the iceberg. All the bad stuff happened out of sight, below the surface.

When Terry had taken over from Frank Murphy, he quickly realised the potential to make a lot of money in the property market. It wasn't long before he had about ten houses at various locations around Runcorn. They were mainly two-up two-down terraces purchased for a song and rented out after throwing a bit of cheap paint over the walls and ceilings. The rent was reasonable compared to other landlords', but he had you by the short and curlies once you settled in. The rent regularly increased without warning until tenants fell behind with their payments.

Chilli liked intimidating people and dealing with rent arrears was one of the many things he helped Terry to sort out. Sometimes a slap across the face would be sufficient to make people pay up. Other times, Chilli offered them a deal that didn't involve violence. Delivering 'parcels' was one way of reducing rent payments, 'parcels' being Chilli's word for drugs. If this wasn't acceptable, tenants were sent to collect rent from other tenants in arrears. It often got them into trouble with their neighbours, but that was their problem. Most people chose the first option.

For single women afraid to deliver parcels or collect rent, he suggested they do him a small 'favour.' There was nothing to lose and if anything untoward happened, it could be denied. He was surprised at how many took him up on his offer. Afterwards, Chilli would call to let Terry know he'd hooked another fish. There had been two suicides and one death in houses rented out by TL Holdings Ltd. They had all been single women.

***

Sandra Fellows always paid her rent on time. Always. When she was made redundant, the thought that she might also lose her home was unbearable. She phoned her landlord who seemed to understand her predicament; she wasn't the first tenant who had fallen on hard times. He would come around to see her and sort something out.

The next day, Terry arrived with Chilli in tow. They sat, listened and nodded as Sandra cried and promised to pay the rent and arrears as soon as she could. She was mortified when Terry stood up and told her to 'pay up or get out.'

They returned a few days later, listened to the same story and watched more tears roll down Sandra's face. Terry suggested she might be able to do them a favour, just the once, to avoid eviction.

'Get out of my house,' Sandra screamed when she realised what he meant.

'Actually, it's my house,' said Terry as he and Chili grabbed hold of her.

She was 49 years old and had a heart condition. They didn't know, and they didn't care.

The post mortem results confirmed that she'd died from a heart attack. It also showed that she'd had sexual intercourse immediately before her death and had sustained both internal and external injuries.

Her neighbours reported seeing Terry and Chilli at the house the day she died. When the police interviewed them, their stories were identical.

'She was okay when we went to visit her and even offered herself as compensation for the unpaid rent. I was surprised, but you don't knock back an offer like that, do you' said Terry.

When asked about the injuries, Terry shrugged. 'It was consensual.'

The police had to let them go due to a lack of evidence.

Eleven

Chilli smiled at the look of fear on Ryan's face and remembered his army days. During a regular training session, he'd landed awkwardly after jumping off a cargo net. The squaddie behind him jumped off the top of the net and landed feet first on Chilli's outstretched arm. It was a messy break with the bone sticking out through the skin. The pain had been excruciating.

He knew how Ryan was going to feel.

Deniability was Terry's reason for leaving the dirty work to Chilli, although there were occasions when Terry preferred to deal with things himself. The first time Chilli witnessed Terry's temper was when he came up against a couple of smart-arsed debt collectors who had strayed into his property business. They'd both ended up in hospital after Terry laid into them.

Chilli was taller and broader than Terry and thought he could handle him in a fight, but he wasn't stupid enough to believe he would walk away without injuries. At the very least, he would probably end up with a broken nose. Chilli's job was to do the dirty work so Terry could remain innocent of all charges without fear of contradiction.

***

Ryan squirmed in the chair like a grandson trying to avoid his moustached grandma's prickly kiss.

'Please, Mr Lynch, it was an accident. I wouldn't hurt nobody's mum, specially not yours. Please don't do this.'

Terry smiled at Chilli, who walked over to Ryan and leant in close to his ear, like a lover whispering sweet nothings.

'Are you right-handed or left-handed?'

Ryan looked at him quizzically, 'right-handed.'

Smiling, Chilli said, 'I'll do you a favour and break your left arm. Do what I say, and it won't get nasty. If you make it difficult, I'll break both your arms.'

Ryan whimpered. 'No, please.'

Twelve

Jackie had often complained about having a sore throat the day after they'd been drinking, but she put it down to all the talking and laughing they'd done the night before. When the sore throat became a persistent cough, Danny persuaded her to see a doctor. Her tests came back positive for throat cancer. They were devastated, but once they'd dried their eyes, they made a pact to get through the treatment, beat the cancer and get on with their lives. It was a difficult time for both of them.

After the chemotherapy, Jackie went for more tests to check on her progress.

The disease had spread to her mouth. Swallowing solid food became almost impossible. The consultant put her on a diet of vitamins and protein shakes.

The young guy who lived in the brand new penthouse upstairs liked to party. They hadn't had a good nights sleep since he moved in a few weeks earlier. The police did nothing to help. A week ago, Danny had knocked on the penthouse door, but the music was so loud no one heard him. He returned later and pushed a note through the letterbox asking for a bit of consideration, but nothing changed.

Thirteen

Ryan was hyperventilating. His breath was coming in short, sharp gasps. His lips were numb like he'd just had an injection of anaesthetic at the dentist. He was close to passing out as the balance between breathing in oxygen and breathing out carbon dioxide altered. His forearm was broken in two places; the bones sticking out of his skin had no right to be there. He'd never seen a broken bone before and was partly repulsed, partly fascinated and just stared at the ends of the bones, which were surprisingly white. *Like toothpaste.* His stomach heaved in protest.

Chilli was pissed off.

'You stupid bastard!' Chilli shouted.

Terry walked over as Chilli pointed at Ryan's left arm tied to the edge of the table. Somehow, Ryan had moved back a few inches as Chilli brought the scaffolding pole down towards his arm, a natural reaction to what was about to happen, but the rope should have prevented any movement. Chilli was all set to make it a simple fracture, but now Ryan needed to have the bones reset. Chilli was able to smack him in the face a couple of times for the hassle he'd just caused them before Terry stepped in and stopped him.

***

It was dark when Chilli abandoned Ryan at the A & E reception desk. The receptionist took Ryan's details and asked him why he was there. He showed her his arm, and the tuna mayo sandwich she'd eaten earlier almost reappeared on the desk in front of her. She showed him the seating area and told him to wait for an orderly to take him to the X-ray department.

In the waiting area after the X-ray, an attractive, long-haired brunette in a white coat with a stethoscope round her neck walked towards him. She looked like a vision from one of his fantasies. The clipboard and glasses completed the illusion. She checked his name, address and date of birth.

'I'm Doctor Coulton,' she said, scribbling something on her clipboard. 'Follow me.' She took him to the triage area and sat him down in one of the cubicles.

'What happened to your arm?'

The mention of his arm was enough to make him forget his fantasy and bring him back to reality. He dropped his head and stared at the floor.

'I kinda tripped on the pavement and fell on the kerb.'

She looked at him doubtfully. 'Who brought you in?'

'My uncle.'

She noticed his cheeks turn red but didn't question him further.

She held the X-rays up to the light. 'Well, it's a bad injury, Ryan. You have a double compound fracture, but it's nothing we can't sort out with a couple of metal plates and a few screws.'

He looked up with a worried frown. 'What you sayin'?'

She sighed and dropped the clipboard to her side.

She was halfway through another double shift, and she'd been dealing with idiots all day. She was tired and hungry and wanted to go home, but that wouldn't be for another eight hours. She'd been flippant with Ryan and unprofessional. It wasn't his fault she was tired. *Pretend it's dad you're talking to.*

'I mean, you'll need surgery for some internal fixation which involves putting your bones back together with metal plates and screws while they heal. We'll have to debride and irrigate the wound first just in case there's some dirt in there, and you'll need a general anaesthetic for the operation, so you'll have to stay in overnight. We'll need to keep an eye on you for 24 hours.'

He looked directly at her for the first time.

'Can't you just put a cast on it so as I can go home?'

His blue eyes held her attention, making her feel uncomfortable. She made a show of checking her notes and took the opportunity to confirm his date of birth. *You're older than you look, but you need to grow up.*

'No, we can't Ryan. The bones sticking out might get infected, and we would have to amputate your arm.'

The mention of amputation had Ryan dry heaving. He spluttered in between the spasms, 'I was only askin'. It really hurts.'

'I bet it does, so let's get you cleaned up and ready for the operation. Any questions?'

'Can I call my mum and let her know I'm here?'

'Won't your uncle tell her?'

He looked away. 'I just want her to know I'm alright.'

'Okay. Have you got a phone, or shall we call her for you?'

'It's in my pocket,' he said, grinning like a schoolboy. 'Can you get it for me?'

She shook her head and laughed. *You definitely need to grow up!* She walked out of the cubicle and asked the nurse to get Ryan ready for surgery.

On Monday, Doctor Coulton came in for another 12-hour shift. Ryan was sat up in bed drinking tea and looked pleased to see her. She confirmed that the operation had been a success.

'The cast can come off in about six weeks, and you'll need physiotherapy to get full movement back in your arm. Keep away from those nasty pavements, Ryan,' she said, smiling as she left.

'They're no good for you.'

Fourteen

Ryan watched as a grey-haired man wearing faded jeans and a dark-blue pinstripe waistcoat over a white shirt walked onto the ward. He looked around the beds and smiled when he saw Ryan.

'Ryan Thomson?' he asked as he stood at the end of the bed.

Ryan nodded.

The man smiled again and approached him. 'Was your dad Jimmy Thomson?' he asked. 'And your mam Sheila?'

'Yes,' Ryan said. 'Who are you?'

'Thought it was you,' he said triumphantly. 'You look a lot like him.'

'How do you know my name?'

'I heard them ask for you outside the X-ray department.'

The stranger held up his bandaged left hand. 'Hit my finger with a hammer and broke it while I was trying to fix a squeaky floorboard. Had to have it reset. They wanted to see if it was lined up properly.'

They stared at one another.

'Ah yes, sorry, forgot to introduce myself; my name's Bernie Martyn. Your mam might have mentioned me.'

Ryan frowned.

Bernie's smile disappeared. 'I used to be best mates with your dad. Me and him grew up together. I knew you when you were a little 'un, about five or six years old. We used to play footie in your garden.'

Ryan stared.

'You don't remember, do you? Never mind. How's your mam?'

Ryan wasn't in the mood for conversation.

'I've never seen you before, and my dad left us when I was six. Sorry but I don't want to talk about him.'

Bernie wasn't put off. 'I just wanted to know if he's okay. I haven't seen him for a long time.'

'How should I know?' Ryan said. 'I haven't heard from him since he left.'

Bernie frowned and stroked his beard. 'That can't be right. I saw him about ten years ago. He said he was writing letters to you all the time. He showed me a picture of you holding up a cup for something you'd won. You were wearing blue shorts and a blue and white running vest. Dead proud he was.'

Ryan remembered the cup he'd won for winning the most 5k races over the school year. His mum had taken the photo. *How did he get hold of it?* 'I didn't get any letters.'

'Well, he said he sent them, so he must have done.'

'He was lying,' Ryan said.

Bernie's shoulders straightened. 'Your dad was a lot of things, but he wasn't a liar. If he said he sent you letters, then trust me, that's what he did.'

'But he left me.'

'Had to,' Bernie said. 'Didn't your mam tell you?'

Ryan shook his head.

Bernie sat down on the bed next to Ryan. 'I'll tell you what I know' he said.

Fifteen

People often described Ryan as 'gangly.' He had longish black hair which hung in his eyes. He had a curious way of looking like he'd just got out of bed – at any time of the day – and his personal hygiene left a lot to be desired. The scar in his left ear lobe was due to a piercing he'd had when he was 17. He thought it would give him some street cred, but one of his mates pulled it out for a laugh and he never thought about getting another one. He decided he didn't like pain.

He slouched a lot and walked like a baby giraffe taking its first steps. He wasn't good at much, but the baby giraffe became a gazelle when he joined the school running team. He was a natural. His stamina and long legs won races. He was set to be a star distance runner, and everyone thought he might get an England call-up one day. Then all his dreams of a bright future came crashing down.

Mr Turner taught history and was considered an 'easy touch' by his class of 16-year-olds because he couldn't control them. It didn't help that most of the boys were taller and broader than him.

The black leather wallet had been a gift from his parents on his graduation day. He'd had it for years. After class, Mr Turner had left it on his desk, and Ryan put it in his pocket. *Simples*. One of the girls had seen him do it and alerted Mr Turner. Ryan was frogmarched to the headmaster's office and told to sit and wait while Mr Turner explained to the headmaster what had happened. They expelled Ryan that day, a week before his exams.

The Board of Governors wouldn't allow him back into the school, so he left without any qualifications. The school wouldn't give him a reference either. He ended up doing odd jobs for people now and then, but the money was never enough to make it worthwhile.

After being expelled, he stopped running competitively. However, his natural ability to put one foot in front of the other faster and for longer than everyone else came in handy in his new 'career.' He began stealing from people to make ends meet. Anyone who chased after him was left far behind in the slipstream of his 6'6" frame. When he ran, his head, back and shoulders were ramrod straight. When he came to a stop his slouched posture returned, and his height dropped a few inches.

People had always looked down on Ryan – figuratively speaking, as he towered over most of them – they all thought they were better than him. They had money, and he didn't, so he tipped the balance back in his favour. He gave most of what he stole to his mum and sister, like a modern-day Robin Hood.

Stealing didn't stop him from having a good night's sleep. There were plenty of other things that did that – his mum and sister, for starters. A couple of his mates had started taking smack and paid him to pick it up for them. It was a shit way to get a bit of extra cash, but sometimes they gave him a bit of the stuff for himself. He gave it to his mum and sister.

Supplying and using drugs meant that he mixed with a lot of unsavoury characters, most of whom were paranoid and would turn on him at the drop of a hat, his sister included. Looking at a dealer the wrong way at a pick-up guaranteed him a kick in the nuts.

His mum enjoyed a drink and recreational drugs now and then, but his sister's drug habit became all-consuming. She didn't pay him, demanded more and wouldn't listen when he told her he needed money to buy the stuff. She laughed at him when he whined about being broke and loved the fact that she could shout and scream at her big brother, and he just took it. She thought all men were like him. She got a wake-up call when one of her boyfriends took exception to her screaming at him and punched her in the face – she calmed down a bit after that.

To keep his sister happy, Ryan had started taking chances to steal whatever he could whenever an opportunity presented itself. He knew it was only a matter of time before he got caught. His luck had run out when he knocked over Terry Lynch's mum on Saturday afternoon.

Ryan left the hospital on Monday afternoon and walked home with one arm in a cast and the other carrying a bagful of antibiotics and painkillers. He didn't have any money for a taxi or a bus, and there was no one to call to pick him up. He'd phoned his mum from the hospital to tell her what had happened, but she wasn't interested. She sounded like she'd had a few cans of the strong, cheap lager she liked. It didn't matter. He wanted to be on his own. He'd had time to think about his life and didn't like how his story was unfolding. Bernie Martyn had told him a lot of good things about his dad, and he wanted to know more. His mum had some explaining to do.

Ryan tried to remember a time when his life wasn't a struggle and came to the conclusion that things had changed when his dad left. Looking back, he could pinpoint exactly when it had gone from bad to worse. Taking Mr Turner's wallet had been a crossroads. That stupid mistake had sent him down a different road. He began to understand that life was full of choices, and he'd made all the wrong ones. *It's time things changed.*

Sixteen

It had been a couple of relatively quiet weeks since Chilli had broken Ryan's arm, but today it was back to business as usual. He had been reliably informed that the Clarendon on Church Street was Danny Valik's local watering hole, which was why he stood at the end of the bar sipping a pint of water. He wasn't there for a beer – he was there on business – although a pint of lager and a whisky chaser would have been very welcome.

It wasn't the first time he'd been to the Clarendon. As always, the décor was shabby, the dusty red carpet hadn't been changed in decades, and paint was peeling off the ceiling. It was in dire need of a makeover. The brewery had tried to update it by installing a beautifully carved oak bar. It was a quality piece of furniture. No doubt they'd blown the whole decorating budget on it but it needed more than a new bar.

Chilli watched as a man wearing a black leather biker jacket and faded blue jeans walked through the door and headed for the bar. He'd seen him before. He remembered elbowing the guy in the face at the flats on Queen Street a few months earlier.

One of the regulars said, 'Hey Danny.'

This was his man. Chilli made eye contact for a couple of seconds and then looked away.

***

Danny just wanted to relax for an hour and get away from everything. It had been two stressful weeks, starting with the attempted robbery of Jackie's bag and the constant visits to the hospital for treatment. He didn't argue when Jackie suggested he go to the Clarendon and catch up with Keith and the regulars. After all, it was Saturday night! He left her under a pile of blankets and pillows on the sofa watching TV.

Danny sat on one of the wooden stools at the bar and ordered a pint of his favourite real ale. He took a mouthful, and his taste buds began to sing. He was holding a glass filled with heavenly nectar, nothing like the chemical crap other people drank these days. Chilli walked over to him and leant in with a wolfish smile.

Keith, the manager, knew Chilli Edwards, the eyes, ears and muscle of Terry Lynch. He wasn't a regular but usually turned up when Terry needed someone to be intimidated. Keith noticed Chilli staring at Danny. He couldn't hear what was said when Chilli sidled up to him, but it looked like a one-way conversation.

'Mr Valik,' Chilli said. 'How's the nose?'

Danny ignored him and paid for the drink in front of him.

Chilli slammed his glass of water onto the bar. 'I've been told to have a word with you, otherwise I wouldn't talk to you in a month of Sundays! I need you to pay attention, so look at me!'

Danny turned and looked him in the eye.

Lowering his voice, Chilli said, 'I understand you live in the flats on Queen Street. Ninth floor, number 9a.'

Danny blinked.

'I also understand you're giving the young lad on the tenth floor a bit of a hard time. Banging on his door at all hours, calling the police and damaging his car.'

'Hang on,' Danny said, 'I don't bang on doors, and I haven't touched his car.'

Chilli ignored him and carried on whispering. 'Stop bothering him, or I'll pay you and Jackie a visit. Understand?'

At the mention of Jackie, Danny began to unconsciously grind his teeth.

He noticed Keith walk to the opposite end of the bar. He looked a bit like Rigsby out of the TV series Rising Damp, but he wasn't as miserable. Danny knew about the baseball bat hidden under the bar. Keith threatened customers with it if things got a bit rowdy on a Saturday night.

Trying not to get riled, he continued to listen. He thought he was doing surprisingly well ignoring the threats until the gorilla suddenly grabbed his arm, and the switch went off in his head.

He was fast for a big guy but not fast enough to avoid the pint glass Danny smashed into the side of his face.

Chilli released his grip and dropped to the floor as the bar fell silent. Danny stood stock-still until Keith broke the silence and shouted 'Run, Danny. Run!'

He ran, managing to avoid the long, gorilla arms that attempted to grab his legs.

The blood dripping into Chillis eyes made it hard to see. By the time he wiped his eyes, Danny was out the door. Furious that he got away, Chilli launched himself at Keith. The baseball bat might just as well have been a fly swatter.

Danny ran left towards the bridge, then turned right past the church where he'd got married, and stopped at the promenade to get his breath back. *Shit, I'm out of shape.* He hadn't been running for a while and tried to bring his heart rate down by using a box breathing technique he'd learnt to help him with his anger issues. After a few minutes, he started to laugh at what had happened. It was like something out of a seventies TV cop show. Glassing someone in the face was a definite first for him.

What the hell just happened? I was doing okay until he threatened Jackie and grabbed my arm, then BOOM!

With the switch in his head turned off and his adrenalin beginning to recede, he got his breath back. *I could do with a drink now!* He laughed again at the absurdity of it.

Seventeen

It hadn't been the best of summers, but Danny couldn't remember the last time it had been a good one. The summers of his childhood were hotter than anything he experienced nowadays. There were odd times when the sun gave off enough heat to make you feel good about yourself, but today hadn't been one of them. Although the air was cool, Danny was still hot and sweaty after his mad dash from the Clarendon.

Music was blasting into the night as he stood at the entrance to the Queen Street block. It was coming from the penthouse. He was not in the mood for yet another Saturday all-nighter.

He walked up the stairs, not wanting to use the lift as he didn't trust the ancient wheels and jittery gears. He was out of breath when he arrived at the ninth floor, his feet bouncing in time to the thump of the bass beat coming from the penthouse above.

He opened the door. 'It's me.'

Jackie turned to him and smiled, then looked up at the ceiling and raised an eyebrow. 'I think there's a party going on upstairs. Any guesses what time we'll get to sleep tonight?'

He sat down next to her on the sofa and kissed her cheek.

'How come you're back so early?' she asked. 'Ah, you didn't want to miss a scintillating Saturday night of second rate TV game shows, did you,' she said, grinning.

She snuggled into him and asked, 'Did you take your Warfarin before you went out?'

'Yes,' he said, 'all done.' He rarely forgot to take it these days, but Jackie always made sure.

Looking at her tired and sunken eyes, he said, 'I'll go up and ask him to turn the music down.'

'Leave it, honey,' she said, gently taking hold of his arm, 'you know it won't make any difference.'

She smiled at him, and tenderly placed her hand in his. She was frail and her weight had plummeted since she'd stopped eating solid food.

He shook his head, grabbed his phone and said, 'I'm going to call the police.'

She let out a world-weary sigh but said nothing.

'I know' he said. 'The police are probably sick of me complaining, but if we don't, nothing will change. They'll have to log the call so they can't say, "We didn't know about it," and I bet no one else has phoned tonight.' He made the call, gave his details and explained the nature of his complaint to the officer. They settled down to watch TV. As mind-numbing as it was, it was nowhere near as bad as the continuous beat of the music coming from upstairs.

After two hours of TV and no sign of the police, he turned to Jackie. 'I can't stand this. You should be sleeping. I'm going up to have a word.'

'Danny, don't. It'll stop in a bit. It's Sunday tomorrow. We can have a lie-in.'

She was making sense, as usual, but as usual, he wasn't listening. He didn't have anything against people enjoying themselves and having parties, but not every night of the week. He stood up and headed for the door. She got up to stop him before he did anything stupid. She made it onto her feet and stood weak-kneed.

'Danny,' she whispered. Her knees buckled beneath her and he just managed to grab her arm before she hit the floor.

'What are you doing? Are you alright?' He helped her to sit back down.

She took a moment before replying, 'I'm okay, just a bit dizzy. I stood up too quickly.' He fetched a glass of water and was happy to see some colour return to her cheeks.

'Don't go up there, Danny,' she pleaded.

He closed his eyes and nodded. 'Alright, but you have to take it easy.'

She smiled and drank the water. He lay her down and made her comfortable.

When she fell asleep, he went upstairs. He banged on the door with the side of his fist as loudly as he could. Unsurprisingly, no one answered, so he continued to hammer away until it finally opened. A young guy stood regarding him with heavy-lidded eyes. The sickly, sweet smell of marijuana clung to him like smoke from a BBQ.

'Are you the tenant?' shouted Danny over the noise.

The guy looked him up and down, then turned and shouted 'Jason! It's for you!'

Jason came to the door bopping his head to the music. 'What's up, granddad.'

'It's Sunday. Turn the music down.'

Jason grinned and cupped a hand to his ear. 'What? I can't hear you!'

'We can't hear ourselves think downstairs and you know my wife's not well. Turn it down!'

'Piss off.'

'I've phoned the police.'

Jason smiled. 'And?'

'And they should be here soon, so why don't you just turn it down and save yourself some bother.'

Jason smiled again. 'Don't worry, granddad. They won't bother me.'

He shut the door in Danny's face.

Danny called the police again.

Eighteen

The police eventually arrived in the early hours and stopped the party. Jason wasn't happy. He stormed downstairs and banged on Danny's door, shouting threats that promised various degrees of pain. Danny held back his temper as he tried to prevent Jason and his mates from forcing their way into his home.

Jackie didn't know how long it would take before Danny's switch kicked in and all hell broke loose. She was weak, nauseous, and scared. Instinctively, she moved towards her safe place – the balcony – to get as far away from the shouting and banging as she could. As she stepped out into the fresh air, she felt dizzy and reached for the handrail to steady herself.

She fell backwards off the ninth-floor balcony, arms outstretched like an opera singer accepting a standing ovation after a perfect performance. She reached for the stars as they watched silently in their shimmering billions.

She thought she heard a woman desperately screaming and realised it was her. *How strange*. She thought of Danny. *I hope he'll be okay.*

Danny heard the scream and turned to see Jackie disappearing over the edge of the balcony. He ran towards her even though he knew he couldn't get to her in time. He let out a grief-stricken howl that echoed across the river, and for a heartbeat, he thought of following her – it would have been easy. He peered over the edge of the balcony and saw the only person he'd ever given his heart to, lying on the ground beneath him. The celestial audience held its collective breath.

He ran out of the flat, pushing Jason and his mates out of the way and descended two steps at a time until he reached ground level. Outside, a crowd of people had gathered around Jackie's body. He headed towards her broken form but slowly came to a halt a few yards from the edge of the crowd. Did he want his last memory of the woman he loved to be a snapshot of her crumpled body lying on the ground surrounded by gawking strangers? The last time he saw her, she had been alive on the sofa. A few women in the crowd had turned away crying. He heard a voice say something about an ambulance as he stared into the distance.

'Danny,' a woman gently touched his arm, snapping him out of his daze. 'There's an ambulance on the way.'

'That's not going to help,' he said with finality.

'What happened?' she asked, looking up.

He slowly lifted his head and looked up at three faces looking down at him from the balcony of his flat.

He marched to the entrance and ran back up the stairs. His anger was a living thing inside him. He didn't know where it would take him, but he didn't care. He got to the ninth floor and charged into his empty flat. *Not here!* He ran up to the penthouse and hammered on the door. After a few seconds, he began kicking it, and when no one answered, he went back down to his flat, got the baseball bat from behind the door and ran back. He swung it at Jason's door a few times and was pleased to see a hole beginning to form in the newly installed UPVC door. He heard angry voices inside, and the door opened. Jason and his two mates crowded into the hallway shouting and swearing.

Danny didn't hesitate. He pushed the guy closest to him into the other two, and they all staggered back into the flat, followed closely by Danny. He swung his foot into the bollocks of the guy he'd just pushed. The other guy to the right of Jason did nothing and held his hands up in surrender.

'Get out!' Danny shouted at him.

The guy turned to Jason, looked back at the baseball bat and without a word, picked up his mate and dragged him out.

Danny turned to Jason. 'Now it's your turn.'

Nineteen

Jason lay on the ground, his left leg at an angle that would have been impossible if it hadn't been broken. Danny had used the bat to good effect. It was a 33" long North American Ash, lightweight and known to flex a little. Lots of hitters used them for that reason.

He'd bought it in one of the second-hand charity shops on the High Street. Jackie was with him at the time and asked him why he was buying it.

'I didn't know you liked rounders, and in case you hadn't noticed, we live in a flat Danny. You're not going to get much use out of it.'

'It's not a rounder's bat, as you very well know,' he said with a grin. 'I just like the look of it. Maybe we could put it up on the wall as a feature.'

She rolled her eyes. He never said that it might come in useful one day for something other than hitting baseballs.

He was right about that, and today was the day. He'd swung it like he'd seen baseball players do many times in films and TV shows. Left leg forward slightly, both hands on the bat, right hand above the left hand and a swing that started behind his right shoulder and ended with a good follow-through. His technique, though not perfect, worked well and broke Jason's leg as easily as a broken promise.

Danny waited until Jason stopped screaming and then phoned for an ambulance. While they waited, Jason got his courage back and threatened Danny with painful torture when his dad found out what had happened.

Danny didn't know anything about Jason or his dad but thought the threats were pathetic. Jason was like a kid doing the 'My dad's bigger than your dad' thing in the playground. Danny ignored him.

An image of Jackie falling off the balcony came to mind. It was all so wrong. She didn't have long to live, but she shouldn't have died like that. They still had a lot to talk about and had recently found themselves reminiscing about all the good things they had done together. They shared a lot of laughs which usually ended in tears of frustration. He'd written some stuff that he wanted to say to her, things that would mean more towards the end. Now he wouldn't get the chance. He hadn't been able to say goodbye.

Jason mouthing off interrupted his thoughts. Danny walked across the room and raised the bat above his head. Jason's eyes went wide and he quicly raised his arm to defend himself.

'Thought that would shut you up, you piece of shit.' Danny lowered the bat. 'Now, keep it shut, or I'll break your arm as well.'

Jason slowly lowered his arm. 'I didn't kill her, so why you acting like I did? She was gonna die anyway.'

Danny's fingers curled tightly around the bat. 'If you had killed her, we wouldn't be having this conversation. You'd be dead. You and your mates came to our flat and frightened her. If you hadn't done that, she'd still be alive.'

Jason said nothing. The wail of an approaching siren broke the silence. Danny didn't know if it had come for Jackie or Jason. He walked back to his flat, head down, dragging the baseball bat behind him.

He went onto the balcony and carefully peered over the edge where the handrail had been. The flashing lights of two ambulances below lit up the small crowd gathered around her. Someone had covered her with a coat. It was surreal.

The image of Jackie disappearing over the balcony came unbidden again. It was going to haunt him for a long time, probably forever. The switch in his head turned off, and his adrenalin levels subsided. Exhaustion and nausea took over.

What was it the gorilla said? 'I've been told to have a word with you.' Someone sent him to tell me to stop bothering Jason. He was pretty sure he would hear from the gorilla's handler again when the news got out about Jason. He couldn't stay at the flat. The police would want to speak to him, the gorilla had his address, and besides, there was no longer any reason for him to stay.

He looked at his watch. He had about five minutes to get out before the police would be all over him. He packed some clothes into an old army rucksack and grabbed his debit card, cash, keys, and bike gear. He was closing the door when he remembered his medication. He got his Warfarin, took one last, slow look around, closed the door and headed down the stairs.

His red Honda VFR 750 was an old girl now, but still his pride and joy. He pushed the heavy machine out of the garage, locked the door and started her up. The engine settled into a low rumble while he zipped up his leather jacket and swung the rucksack onto his back. Before he could put his helmet and gloves on, he heard voices and saw two figures come around the corner from the entrance to the flats. *Jason's mates!* He jumped on the bike, put his arm through the helmet's chin guard, gunned the throttle, and accelerated towards them. They tried to kick him off as he passed, but he stayed upright and made it onto Church Street. He headed towards the traffic light junction a hundred yards away.

The lights were red, so he stopped and took the opportunity to put his helmet on. No point drawing attention to himself. He checked the fuel gauge and noticed the digital clock next to it.

3am. So much for a quiet night at the Clarendon! The lights changed to green, and he headed for the dual carriageway that led to the M56 Motorway and North Wales.

Twenty

Terry sat on the sofa late Saturday evening with a glass of his favourite 18-year-old Macallan Scotch Whisky and watched as Karen paced up and down the room. They'd been married 25 years, and although they didn't always see eye to eye, she'd been a good wife as far as he was concerned. Their two children were now in their twenties and Karen had done her best to raise them right. Emma was 24 and had trained as a solicitor with the sole purpose of joining the family business. She was smart and made her parents proud. Jason was a couple of years younger and had been a problem for Terry for at least 15 of his 22 years.

Jason was a mummy's boy and often got Terry's back up. He was rebellious and stubborn and wanted to prove himself all the time. Although of average height and build, he always picked fights with bigger guys. Things didn't usually end well for mummy's blue-eyed boy when he picked on Terry's men.

Terry also found out that Jason was trying to make a name for himself by fighting some of the local young bulls who fancied their chances against 'Terry Lynch's boy.' It was becoming an unnecessary hassle that Terry could do without, so he moved his son away from Liverpool into the newly refurbished tenth-floor penthouse flat in Runcorn, under the watchful eye of Chilli. In the meantime, he had the problem of Sophie to deal with.

'Sophie is becoming a big problem,' said Karen. 'You've had to let good men go because of her, including Chilli. How many more are going to succumb to her sexual charms?' Terry didn't answer.

Sophie's desire for good looking, dangerous men was detrimental to him and his family. He'd started thinking about hiring ugly men hoping that Sophie wouldn't be interested, but offering someone a job because they were ugly was ridiculous. What mattered was how good they were at their job, not how good they looked whilst doing it. He snorted and shook his head

Karen stopped mid-rant. 'What's so funny?'

'Nothing. I was just thinking about employing ugly men.'

She gave him a disbelieving look and carried on pacing. He watched her and smiled as she marched around the room, waving her hands about like an aircraft marshaller parking planes at a busy airport.

The situation was tricky because Sophie was Gary's wife. Both Terry and Gary had spoken to her, but her slutty behaviour continued.

When Karen paused for breath, he took the opportunity to suggest that it might be better if she had a word with Sophie, woman to woman. She stopped pacing and folded her arms.

'She won't take any notice of you, Terry, so what makes you think the slag will listen to me?'

Terry loved seeing her angry. It made her even more beautiful. Her brown shoulder-length hair, full red lips and high cheekbones accentuated the fire in her eyes. She reminded him of Wonder Woman at times like this. She continued with her tirade.

'I've had enough of her trying her best to pull this family apart.' She went back to striding around the room in magnificent splendour.

Terry couldn't take his eyes off her.

'I don't know how Gary puts up with her or why he keeps on taking her back.' She was in full flow now, the words tumbling out of her mouth. 'How many times has she shagged one of your men, and Gary's done nothing about it? He's a spineless dick if you ask me.'

Terry loved his wife, but sometimes she wound him up tighter than Superman's undies. He'd listened with amusement, but now his smile disappeared.

He turned to her and said quietly, 'I was not asking you.'

The malevolence in his voice was enough to let her know she'd overstepped the mark. Terry wouldn't hear a bad word said about his family, especially his brother, and talking about him like that was unacceptable. She should apologise, but he hated weakness in people and would have thought less of her if she had.

She lowered her voice and changed her tone. 'So what are we going to do about her?'

Even though she hadn't wanted to, she had stepped down from her soapbox; it wasn't much of an apology, but it was the best he was going to get from her. Terry's anger ebbed away.

'Gary and I will come up with something that'll stop this happening again.'

She didn't look convinced.

His phone vibrated in his pocket.

'Speak of the devil,' he said, holding the phone up for Karen to see. 'Gary, we were just talking about you. We need to get together for that chat.' Terry listened. 'Yes,' he said, 'it is becoming a problem. We should get together sooner rather than later to discuss it.'

***

Terry was asleep when his phone rang in the early hours of the morning. It was Gary.

'What now? It's Sunday morning. Do you know what time it is?'

There was a pause, and Terry sat up in bed.

'When was this?' Another pause. 'Which hospital? We're on our way. Call your contacts. Get me a name! I'll give Chilli a call and see if he knows anything.'

He turned to Karen.

'Get up. It's Jason.'

Karen grabbed his arm. 'What's happened?'

He put his hand up in a calming gesture. 'He's in hospital with a broken leg. Get dressed.'

The fear in her eyes subsided as she took a deep breath, relieved that he was alive. She'd come to expect the worst when Terry spoke about hospitals on his phone.

'How did he break it?'

'He didn't. Some guy beat him up with a baseball bat.'

'What! He was attacked? Why?'

'Just get your coat, and we'll go and ask him.'

Fifteen minutes later, they were on the motorway heading for the hospital.

***

Jason was being prepared for surgery in a private room. Terry and Karen made sure he was okay and asked him lots of questions. Like a bad poker player, Jason had a tell when he lied or tried to hide something. Terry observed the first finger and thumb on Jason's left hand tapping together at the side of his leg. Terry's theory was that the tapping mirrored Jason's heartbeat. The more significant the lie, the faster the tapping became.

Jason's story appeared to be partially true, but he was holding something back.

Some guy had banged on his door, marched into his flat and broken his leg. *Why would someone do that and then phone an ambulance?*

Jason would be in hospital for a couple of days before going home. Karen insisted that he stay with them until he got back on his feet. Although Terry's relationship with Jason wasn't the best, he didn't want to upset Karen so he agreed.

Before they left, Jason told his dad the name of his attacker.

Danny Valik. I'm going to find you, Mr Valik, and when I do, you'll wish I hadn't.

Twenty-One

There wasn't much traffic on the roads heading into North Wales at that time of the morning. Danny turned off the A55 dual carriageway at junction 23 for Llandullas and stopped at the service station. He rang Colin, a mate from his school days who was 'topping up his tan' in Spain. Danny told him what had happened to Jackie, and before Colin had the chance to throw a truckload of questions at him, Danny asked if he could stay at the caravan up in the Welsh hills for a while. Colin said he wasn't planning on returning to the UK any time soon, so it would be okay.

'Speak to Megan, the site owner and mention Sheba, the German Shepherd.'

'Wasn't Sheba your dad's dog when we were at school?'

'Well remembered. Sheba is our password. Megan has a spare key for the caravan. Stay as long as you like, mate.' Danny thanked him and promised he would be in touch.

He got back on the bike and headed up the long hill that ran parallel to the dual carriageway, the exhaust echoing off the stone walls on either side of the road. He passed the Indian restaurant where he and Jackie had shared onion bhajis and poppadoms, lamb rogan josh and aloo gobi. *Good times.* He took a left turn through a run-down council estate and turned right onto Tan-Y-Graig Road. He accelerated past the derelict Castle Inn, where he and

Jackie had enjoyed drinks and lock-ins with the locals. He passed St Cynfran Church and turned off the road into Mountain View Caravan Park.

At the reception office, he was surprised to find a petite brunette about his age smiling at him.

'I'm a bit of an insomniac' she said. 'Just catching up with some admin stuff before I try and get to sleep. I'm Megan. How can I help?'

'I'm Danny. Caravan number 15 belongs to my mate Colin.'

'And?'

'You still having problems with Sheba, the German Shepherd?'

She smiled and found the key for him.

He thanked her. 'Are you friends with Colin too?'

She blushed a little. 'Yes, we're friends, and you're very honoured. You're only the second person in ten years to ask about Sheba.'

'Is it alright to leave the bike outside reception tonight? I don't want to wake anyone up.'

'Of course,' she said and went back to her admin.

Colin's caravan was as he remembered it from numerous summer holidays with Jackie when they were younger. It was clean and tidy with two small bedrooms, a shower and a kitchen. He found clean sheets and a duvet, made the bed and fell into a deep, exhausted sleep. He dreamt of Jackie falling in slow motion, her long blonde hair swirling around her head, eyes wide with shock and her arms reaching out for him.

He was a fingertip away from saving her when he woke.

The sun was coming up across the caravan park when he looked out of the window. Perfect weather for a Sunday morning jog. Danny put on a t-shirt and jeans and got his trainers from the bottom of his rucksack. It was a crisp autumn morning, and the fresh air filled his lungs.

He'd started running at school and kept it up when he left. He liked the solitary nature of running alone and used the time to clear his head.

In his late-thirties, Danny's stamina had deteriorated rapidly and Jackie eventually persuaded him to see a doctor. An echocardiogram revealed a life-threatening anomaly in his heart. The doctors couldn't believe he was still walking around, never mind running. He had a faulty heart valve and a distended aorta. The consultant at the hospital advised him that his level of fitness had very likely saved his life. He told Danny to stop exercising until after his operation.

They cut him open, inserted a mechanical valve into his heart and repaired the damaged aorta. He would have to take blood thinners for the rest of his life, but it was a small price to pay considering the alternative. That had been three years ago, and he hadn't tried running again until now.

The peacefulness and views across the hills energised him. He loved it. He found it hard to get into a rhythm at first and the jolts of pain through his knees forewarned him of the struggle he would have getting out of bed tomorrow. His head cleared, leaving space for the decisions he was going to have to make.

He reckoned he'd done about four miles by the time he got back to the caravan. He showered and changed, then phoned Sue. When Danny told her what had happened, she burst into tears. She and Jackie were in the same class at school and had become lifelong friends. She couldn't speak, and Danny was on the verge of breaking down. He promised to phone her back later and quickly ended the call.

***

'Are you okay?' He asked when he called again.

'I'm not sure,' said Sue. 'How are you?'

Danny sighed. 'A lot happened yesterday. I'm still trying to take it all in.'

He told her about the Clarendon, how Jackie had died and what he'd done to Jason. She asked if he'd spoken to the police. He hadn't. He presumed the police would get Jackie's details from someone in the crowd.

Sue asked if he needed anything. 'My wife,' he said after a pause and hung up before he broke down completely. He texted her, apologised and said he just needed some time.

Church bells were ringing out across the Welsh hills reminding him of being at home with Jackie. He headed for the local shop and bought some supplies. Megan was in the reception area and waved to him when he returned. He waved back and strolled to the caravan.

Twenty-Two

The police station was a concrete box next to a concrete courthouse, a concrete shopping precinct and concrete council offices. People complained about the monstrosities when they were being built and the architects eventually admitted they'd probably used 'a bit too much' concrete in their design. To compensate for the dull, grey frontage they covered everything in white tiles, which made everything look bland and sterile.

At 9 am, Detective Constable Steve Richards stood at the free vending machine in the police station canteen waiting for his much anticipated third cup of sweet black coffee. He was obsessed with coffee and wondered if he was becoming a caffeine addict. He watched as his boss, Detective Inspector Harry Latchford, approached the vending machine for his first drink of the day.

In the six months since Steve had been promoted to detective, he had never seen his boss wearing anything other than a smart suit, a tie and his legendary shiny black leather shoes – polished daily to perfection. The machine provided Harry with a cup of herbal tea that smelt remarkably like an upmarket aftershave. Steve waited for Harry to start a conversation but gave up when it became apparent, as usual, that it wasn't going to happen.

'Morning, Sir. How are you today?'

'I'm okay, thanks, Steve. How are things with you?'

Harry was a nice guy, but sometimes Steve just wanted to shout, 'Wake up!'

Instead, he followed the script. 'Okay, I suppose, for a Sunday morning. What's today's itinerary, Sir?'

Harry took a sip of his aftershave and pushed his black-rimmed glasses back onto the bridge of his nose.

'There are a couple of things. One report we've had states that in the early hours of this morning, a man was attacked by someone with a baseball bat at the flats on Queen Street. The victim sustained bruising to his arms and a broken leg. Not something we usually deal with, I know. We have to take his statement; he wants his alleged assailant prosecuted.'

Steve took a pen and notebook from his coat and began writing.

The inspector continued. 'The second report concerns the suspicious death of a woman who fell from the ninth floor of the same flats at around the same time. We don't know the details yet.'

Steve stopped scribbling. He'd been a teenager at the time of the last suspicious death in town. It was big news back then, and everybody had talked about it. Harry had been the detective sergeant instrumental in gathering the evidence that led to the arrest and subsequent conviction of a man that murdered his wife. That was how he gained his promotion to detective inspector. Harry had the respect of his colleagues, something Steve hoped to emulate one day.

'Was it suicide?' His pen was bouncing up and down between his fingers.

Harry sat back while Steve got the procedural questions out of the way. He was pleased with the way Steve's training had progressed over the last six months.

'We don't know yet. We'll ask a few questions today and hopefully get some answers.'

Steve nodded excitedly. Finally, something to get their teeth into, a welcome change from the petty thefts and neighbour disputes they usually dealt with.

'What time did these events take place, Sir?'

'The paramedic report states that the woman died at 2.29 am.'

Steve was writing again. 'And the broken leg?'

'The second ambulance crew reported in at 2.53 am.'

Steve took his time, his thought processes doing overtime.

'Which floor?'

'Tenth,' Harry said, taking a sip of his tea.

Steve stopped writing. 'Jason Lynch?'

The scattered pieces of a giant jigsaw puzzle were coming together in his head.

The inspector hoped his protégé would progress onto more complicated puzzles. If Steve kept up this pace, it was likely he would fill Harry's shoes one day.

'The very same.'

'Are the two incidents related, Sir?'

'That's what we're going to find out, detective.' said Harry with a smile. 'Jason Lynch is in hospital. He had an operation this morning to set his leg. A guy called Danny Valik is accused of breaking it and he lives on the ninth floor. It was his wife, Jackie, who fell and died.'

Steve was listening intently and trying to write at the same time. All sorts of scenarios and questions came into his head.

Harry continued. 'We'll visit the flats today and get a statement from Mr. Valik, carry out a door knock, and see if anyone knows anything that might help our investigation. Then we'll go to the hospital and talk to Jason Lynch.' He stood up and pointed at Steve's drink. 'Finish your excuse for a coffee, and we'll head out. We're under pressure from the Assistant Chief Constable to sort this out as soon as possible so all our other investigations are on hold.'

Steve put his pen and notebook away. 'I wonder what the inimitable Terry Lynch will have to say about this.'

Twenty-Three

Danny phoned Sue after falling asleep for most of the afternoon. 'The police called earlier,' she said, 'asking questions about what happened last night. I told them I already knew about Jackie, and they asked me where you were. I said I didn't know. Danny, they're investigating Jackie's death.'

'Good! Jackie shouldn't have died like that. I reported my concerns about the balcony months ago. In fact, I reported it loads of times.'

His voice became a whisper. 'What those lads did was unforgivable.'

Sue hesitated. 'The police want to interview you. A man claims that you smashed a beer glass in his face, and one of your neighbours has accused you of breaking his leg. The officers name is Detective Inspector Latchford. I'll text you his number. You should speak to him.'

Danny said he would think about it.

'Why don't you come and stay here with me while Mike's away?' she said.

***

Sue rang Mike who was somewhere in the North Sea, not far from Scotland, working on one of the oil rigs. She asked him how soon he could get home. After 15 years of marriage, Mike heard the urgency in his wifes voice.

'Sue, the first flight back to the mainland is on Friday. There are storms forecast for the next few days and Friday is the first scheduled flight back. I'm sorry but I'm stuck here until then. Tell me what's happened. Are you okay?'

She told him about Jackie, Jason and the police looking for Danny.

Mike was shocked. 'I can't believe it. Jackie's dead?' He shook his head trying to take it in. 'How are you holding up?'

'I'm not good, to be honest, but Danny's worse. I have no idea what's going on in his head, and I'm scared he's going to do something stupid.'

***

Keith Evesham had lived in Runcorn all his life. He was born, schooled, employed and married there. He was happy working at the spice factory on the industrial estate and never imagined he would work anywhere else. Money was tight after he married and had a couple of kids, so to make ends meet, he helped out in his local pub, the Navigation on Canal Street. He enjoyed the work, and the customers seemed to like him.

He pulled pints for about a year until one of the regulars told him that the Clarendon on Church Street was looking for bar staff. It was a bit more money, so he applied and got the job. Then the spice factory closed down and made him redundant. He worked most days and weekends in the pub while while he looked for another full-time job. Not long after, the brewery began recruiting people to train as managers in their pubs. He applied and passed the application.

He stayed on at the Clarendon for another couple of years as a trainee manager then the old manager retired, and the brewery offered him the job. He'd been full-time manager there for twenty years now and couldn't have been happier.

Jackie and Danny were his favourite regulars, although Danny could get a bit rowdy after a few pints, and customers would ask Keith to have a word with him. He'd grimace, get his baseball bat from behind the bar and point it at Danny. The following day, Danny would always phone to apologise. Keith didn't mind as long as everyone had a good time and bought beer.

Keith was glad Danny was a friend and not an enemy. He'd often witnessed Mr Happy become Mr Angry quicker than a Ferrari going from 0–60. It was instantaneous, and you never knew when it was going to happen. Fortunately, Jackie was usually on hand to calm things down. Danny had often helped him out when petty arguments between customers became drunken fights and after seeing how he dealt with those idiots he wouldn't want to try and throw Danny out of the pub.

***

That evening, Danny finally found the time to think about the implications of what he'd done. If you looked at it in black and white, then, yes, he'd glassed someone in the face and broken someone's leg, but it wasn't black and white as far as he was concerned.

The gorilla had been aggressive, as had Jason and his mates. Jackie was dying from cancer – *no, Jackie is dead*. The tightness deep in his chest threatened to overwhelm him. He decided the best thing to do would be to sort it out with the police and accept whatever punishment came his way.

Danny phoned the mobile number Sue had sent to him. 'Hi, my name is Danny Valik. Is this Detective Inspector Latchford?'

'Yes, thanks for calling Mr Valik. We need to speak to you about certain allegations that have been made against you. Can you come to the station?'

'I'm going to be staying with my sister. You can speak to me there.'

'When?'

'In the next couple of days. I'll give you a call when I'm there. Sue told me you're the officer investigating my wife's death. How's it going?'

There was a slight pause. 'It's coming along. I'll be able to tell you more when I see you.'

***

On Tuesday, Terry phoned one of his police contacts and called in a favour. He found out that Danny had a sister who lived in town. He sent one of his men to the address to keep an eye on her.

Twenty-Four

Danny phoned Inspector Latchford when he arrived at Sue's house on Wednesday, and it wasn't long before there was a knock at the door. Two men in suits were holding ID cards out in front of them like a couple of kids coming home from school with their first school report. The older one said, 'I'm Detective Inspector Latchford and this' – he nodded at his colleague – 'is Detective Constable Richards. Is Mr Valik here?'

Danny leant forward for a closer look at their ID cards. When he was satisfied he said 'I'm Danny Valik. Come in.'

Danny could tell that the inspector was a career policeman. He had an air of confidence about him that could only have come through years of experience. DC Richards, however, looked a little uncomfortable.

'Is that your bike outside?' asked DC Richards. Danny nodded.

'Nice. I always wanted a VFR.' said the young detective taking out his notebook.

The inspector cleared his throat as if to say something, then paused as Sue came into the room and sat opposite him. She crossed her legs and folded her arms.

'Is there a problem, Inspector?'

'No, not at all, as long as Danny doesn't mind you being here.'

The inspector looked over the rim of his glasses at Danny.

'She stays.'

The inspector nodded. 'If you feel up to it, we've got a couple of questions regarding what happened the night your wife died.'

The inspector continued. 'We've received a complaint from a man who alleges that you broke his leg with a baseball bat.'

He waited for a reaction from Danny, but when there wasn't one, he continued.

'We've also received a report stating that you smashed a beer glass into the side of a man's face in the Clarendon on Church Street last saturday night . Would you like to comment on these allegations, Mr Valik?'

Danny looked at the inspector patiently for a few seconds. 'Can you tell me how the investigation into my wife's death is progressing?'

The inspector shuffled uncomfortably on the sofa. 'The investigation is ongoing. Hopefully, what you tell us now will shed some light on the matter. Can you comment on the allegations made against you? Are they true?'

Danny looked at the detectives. *Something doesn't feel right*. 'Did they tell you why I did what I did?'

At a nod from the inspector, DC Richards flicked through his notebook and read out what they'd been told by the victim. 'I asked him to pass me a beer mat, and he smashed a pint glass in my face.'

Danny waited for more, but DC Richards closed his notebook.

'Is that it? He asked me to pass him a beer mat so I smashed a glass in his face? That doesn't make sense does it Inspector. He's lying. And what about the other complaint? Did I break Jason's leg because he wouldn't give me a neighbourly cup of sugar?'

'So you admit to breaking the leg of someone called Jason? ' said the Inspector. 'It's just that we haven't mentioned any names yet? Jason Lynch said you came into his flat with a baseball bat and attacked him for no reason.'

'That's not what happened.' Danny was only just managing to keep his temper at bay.

'There are two witnesses who have given statements to that effect, Danny.'

'Jason's numnut mates, you mean?' he said with derision. 'They're lying. Did you get a statement from the manager at the Clarendon? He'll tell you that the guy in the pub had been aggressive and grabbed my arm. I was defending myself.'

'Keith Evesham? Not yet. When we went to see him on Sunday, his wife told us he was in bed recovering from a beating and was in no shape to give a statement – nor did he want another beating for talking to the police. She wouldn't say who had assaulted him.'

It must have been the gorilla. Danny blamed himself for Keith getting hurt. The bad feeling he had about the direction the interview was taking got worse. He stared at the inspector.

'You've said a couple of times that what I tell you will help sort out the investigation into Jackie's death. My formal statement will say that I was arguing with Jason and his mates outside my flat, and the next thing I know, Jackie fell off the balcony. Will that help?'

DC Richards turned to the inspector, and something unspoken passed between them. The inspector turned to Danny.

'If that's your statement, then we'll have to ask you to come to the station for a recorded interview, under caution.'

Sue frowned. 'A recorded interview. Why? He's just told you what happened.'

Danny was sure something was amiss. 'Has anyone else said anything about my wife's death?'

The inspector cleared his throat. 'Jason and his mates claim that you pushed your wife off the balcony.'

There was a stunned silence.

Sue began to laugh. 'That's so stupid. You obviously don't know how much my brother and his wife love each other, Inspector.'

Sue continued. 'He would never, could never, hurt Jackie. Take it from me. There are a lot of jealous people out there who would give anything to have what they've got, me included.'

Sue stopped when she realised what she'd said. 'To have what they had' she whispered.

'Do you believe them?' Danny asked the Inspector.

'We're looking into it. There were bruises on her arm where someone had grabbed hold of her. You fled the scene before the police arrived. The coroner's preliminary verdict is that Jackie's death is suspicious.'

Danny shook his head and stood up. He knew how it looked, but he wanted to hear it. 'Are you telling me that I'm under suspicion for the murder of my wife?'

'Yes,' the inspector said. 'Can I—'

'No, you can't,' said Sue, standing up. 'You just accused my brother of killing his wife. Get out of my house!'

DC Richards stood and headed towards the hallway but the inspector didn't move. 'You'll have to come to the station, Danny,' said the inspector, ignoring Sue.

Sue insisted that they leave, and as the inspector stood up, she took his elbow and guided him down the hallway. 'You have to attend the police station at 2 pm tomorrow for a formal, recorded interview' he said. Sue opened the front door. 'If you don't attend—' he turned to Danny, '_a warrant will be issued for your arrest.' Sue slammed the door behind them.

***

She began to cry. 'What's going on Danny? You've never been in trouble like this before.' She gently bit her lip. 'It sounds awful – what you did to those men.'

He sighed and said sheepishly, 'Yes, I know it does, but it didn't happen the way they tell it. I'm being set up and saying that I killed Jackie—' His head went down. 'How could anyone say that. I couldn't.'

Sue grabbed hold and squeezed him. 'No one will ever believe that. They're just using the other incidents to make a case against you.'

She let go of him and took a deep breath. 'What happens now?'

He straightened his shoulders and took her hand. 'I don't know, but right now, it's not the police I'm worried about.'

Sue looked puzzled. 'What do you—'

A knock at the door made them both jump.

***

Frank Wharton had been sitting in the silver Ford Mondeo opposite the address Terry had given him for close to 24 hours. The Mondeo wouldn't win any awards for comfort or style but was the most inconspicuous car he could get his hands on at such short notice. Terry told him to grab Danny Valik if he showed up; he hadn't yet, which was okay. Frank was a patient man. He'd been on surveillance operations before, usually in the back of Transit vans, sleeping, eating and shitting in a van for days on end because he couldn't risk being seen. A warm car with windows was heaven, although there wasn't much room for his sizeable frame. Frank was taller and broader than his mate Chilli Edwards.

He had his electronic book reader with him to pass the time, and dozens of books waiting to be read. He was half way through the latest Jack Reacher story. He liked the idea of a vigilante hero, however experience had taught him that firepower and numbers eventually won over in any confrontation.

He was settling into a new chapter when he heard the growl of a bike exhaust and watched as a red Honda stopped in front of the womans house. He wrote down the registration number as the rider killed the engine and got off. It could be Danny Valik, but Frank never jumped to conclusions, which was one of the reasons Terry trusted him with surveillance work. Surveillance required a clear, calm head. Making presumptions that later proved wrong was why some of Terrys men were no longer allowed to do it. Terry avoided situations where innocent people could get hurt because one of his men had made an assumption.

The biker removed his helmet and combed his dark brown mop of hair with his fingers. A woman ran from the house with her arms outstretched.

Frank opened his laptop and connected to an unsecured wifi network in the area. He sent an email with the registration number of the bike to his contact. It would only take a minute to get all the required information. He ended his email with a reminder to send a photograph as the biker might not be the registered keeper. Next, he sent a text to Terry asking for backup. Frank could probably manage on his own, but why take the chance? Anything could go wrong. He returned to Reacher as they went inside.

***

They were having a late breakfast when Terry got Frank's text. He went into the garden to call Chilli. 'We've found him. Call Frank and tell him you're on your way to give him a hand, then get the guy to the unit. And Chilli, I can't talk to him if you put him in hospital, so don't.'

Jason and Karen were sitting at the dining table when he returned. 'Have they found him?' Jason asked with a hint of excitement in his voice.

Terry didn't particularly like his son, and had never admitted it to anyone but himself. Jason had become a headstrong, whingeing bully, similar to a lot of idiots he'd dealt with over the years. Terry knew the type and wouldn't allow Jason to take over the family business until there was a drastic change in his attitude. Gary was the only other option, which brought its own set of problems.

'Yes, we've found him,' Terry said.

'Great!' Jason said with childish glee. 'Now we can do him some damage. I'm gonna enjoy breakin' his legs!'

Terry glared at him and shook his head. 'You are not going anywhere near him. The less you're involved, the better for everyone.'

Karen looked from her son to her husband as Jason got up and hobbled away. Terry gave him a look of disgust as he left the room. The last few days had been difficult for all of them.

Twenty-Five

When Ryan woke on Wednesday morning, something had changed. He couldn't put his finger on it, but it felt like there wasn't enough space for three people in the house anymore. It suddenly felt like Waterloo train station during the morning rush hour.

When he first arrived back from the hospital, he saw his bedroom in a different light. He had the smallest of the three bedrooms, despite being the biggest in the family, and it was a shit-hole. The grimy curtains were closed and the bed unmade. Dirty laundry, used cups, and empty takeaway boxes lay scattered on the floor. He couldn't remember the last time he'd changed the sheets on his bed. It stank. He opened the window and let in some fresh air.

Over the last week or so, Ryan found solace in the small, hilly woodland at the top of Greenway Road that overlooked the river. If he sat on the sandstone outcrop overhanging the hill, he could see the cars crossing the bridge off to his right and the planes landing at Liverpool John Lennon airport ahead in the distance. Somebody had once told him that the pilots knew their landing approach was on track when they cut across the top of the bridge, exactly in the middle of the arch. He looked forward to going there every day, away from the house.

Today he watched as the planes continuously took off and landed. The slight breeze and fresh October air made it into a kind of meditation, and he found a calm place inside himself that he didn't know existed.

He held up his broken arm and stared at it, remembering how terrified and helpless he'd felt as Chilli swung the pole towards him. He hated the thought that he couldn't protect himself. *People have used me all my life, and I'm not havin' it anymore. The world is full of wolves who take advantage of people like me. Well, no more!* It was at that moment, sitting on the rock, legs dangling mid-air, Ryan realised that if things were going to change he was going to have to make some tough choices. He stood up and took a lungful of air that somehow tasted sweeter. He smiled.

***

Chilli walked up to the Mondeo and tapped on the passenger window. The door unlocked, and he squeezed in next to Frank.

'Long time no see Chilli Pepper,' Frank said, happy to see his mate. 'What the hell happened to your face?'

Chilli looked straight ahead. 'The prick that we're going to pick up smashed a pint glass into it.'

'What! And he's still walking around? That doesn't sound like you. Is working in this backwoods town slowing you down, Mate? You losing your touch?'

Chilli grinned and then grimaced as the wounds reminded him of the scars he would carry for the rest of his life. He was going to make sure his revenge was just as painful and unforgettable for Danny Valik.

Frank was staring at him. 'You okay? You're miles away. I just asked you what you're reading at the moment?'

'Sorry, mate. Yeh, I'm okay.'

They'd worked for Terry for a long time and respected each other. Their mutual love of books had cemented their friendship.

'Lord of the Rings,' Chilli said.

Frank smiled. 'Is it that time of year again?'

Chilli had read Lord of the Rings when he was a teenager and something about it struck a chord with him. It could have been the camaraderie of the Fellowship or the affirmation of good defeating evil. Whatever it was had made an impression on him and he made sure he read it every year.

'What have you got there?' Chilli asked, seeing the electronic reader in Frank's lap.

'Jack Reacher. Number 22, The Midnight Line.'

Now it was Chilli's turn to smile.

'You've got a bit of a soft spot for him, haven't you? Don't deny it, Frankie baby,' he said, grinning.

Frank smiled. Then it was down to business – planning the capture of Danny Valik.

***

Danny looked at Sue. 'Are you expecting someone?'

She shook her head.

'Do you still have the nine iron?' he asked.

'By the door, but Danny—'

He saw the fear in her eyes and smiled reassuringly.

'The inspector's probably forgotten something. Just answer the door.'

She passed him the golf club, and he raised it over his shoulder.

She turned the handle and was immediately pushed back into the hallway. A huge man with a shiny, bald head and a grey goatee beard burst through the door. As Sue fell, she caught the front of his foot, making him stumble slightly.

Danny saw an opportunity and before the guy could recover, he swung the club. There wasn't much room in the hallway, but that worked to his advantage. *Fancy that! Same motion, same feeling as the baseball bat!* It connected with the guy's ribs, and Danny was rewarded with the satisfying sound of a breaking bone. The big guy stopped mid-stride, landed on one knee, and started taking short breaths to lessen the pain in his ribs. He looked up at Danny, standing over him with the club up in the air ready to strike again.

'You sonofa_' he rasped, attempting to stand up.

Danny brought the club down onto his outstretched wrist. There was a grunt as the wrist went limp, and the guy went down again.

'Stay down!' shouted Danny, the club up behind his shoulder again.

'Sue, are you alright?' he yelled as she got up off the floor.

She nodded. 'I'm alright.'

'Have you seen this guy before?'

Sue took a good look at the man kneeling in her hallway.

'Yes. I saw him sitting in that silver car when you arrived. I thought he was waiting for someone.'

'Call the police,' Danny said. 'Inspector Latchford won't be far away.'

Sue made the call.

Danny watched the guy kneeling in front of him. He was built like a prop forward and had moved like he was launching into a scrum. Frank glared at Danny nursing his wrist like a mother holding a baby.

'You like breaking bones, don't you. You starting to enjoy it Danny?'

He knows my name! Danny would have hit him again, but he was in enough trouble. Self-defence is one thing, but the people who make the rules frown on excessive force.

'Sue!' shouted Danny. 'Shut the door!'

The gorilla was striding up the path headed towards the house. She turned and slammed the door just in time. His shoulder smashed into it as his momentum carried him forward. The hinges and locks weren't happy, but they held. The continuous hammering on the door was pure frustration. They all looked up at the sound of a police siren in the distance. Danny was right; Inspector Latchford hadn't been far away.

***

Chilli got the spare keys from behind the sun visor in the Mondeo and drove it around the corner out of the way. He watched as two police cars arrived and took Frank away in handcuffs. There was no chance of attempting a rescue.

The plan was supposed to be foolproof. Frank would go through the front door and grab Danny. Chilli would go around the back to stop any chance of escape.

When Chilli didn't hear from Frank, he went to the front of the house. He saw Frank kneeling in the hallway holding his wrist, Danny standing over him with a golf club in his hand and the sister talking on her mobile. Instinct took over as he headed towards the door, but a shout from Danny alerted the woman, and he couldn't get inside. When Chilli heard the siren, he ran back to the car. *No point in both of us getting caught.* Now he had to tell Terry that Frank had been arrested and Danny wouldn't be available for a chat any time soon. He got the story straight in his head and made the call.

Twenty-Six

Danny was rubbing the scar over his right eye. 'I can't stay here any longer, Sue. I don't want you in the firing line. The gorilla and his mate will come back if they know I'm here. I would if I were them. Jason, no doubt, will be looking for me when his leg heals. It's too dangerous for you. I'm going to see Keith, he may know something, and then I'll go back to Wales.'

'Why don't you let the police handle it?' she asked, knowing that once he'd made up his mind, no one other than Jackie could change it.

'I don't think the police can help me, and besides, I don't trust them. I'll speak to a few people and let you know how I get on.'

He grabbed his gear and left for the Clarendon, his head full of questions. *Who's the bald guy with the goatee, and what does he want with me? I get why Chilli was there. Are they working together?*

His conversation with Keith had been awkward. He'd been beaten pretty badly and had shuffled around the Clarendon like an old man. Danny tried to apologise, but Keith waved it away. They sat in a quiet corner at the side of the bar, and Keith told him what had happened.

'After you ran out, Chilli came for me and started throwing stools and glasses around. I had my baseball bat and hit him across his shoulder, but it just bounced off him. He grabbed the bat and hit me a few times. He didn't use it on my head or face. He used his fists for that. '

Keith's black eyes and crooked nose were testament to that.

'I'm really sorry, Keith. I didn't think he'd go for you.'

Keith tried to smile. 'I know, but don't worry. I'll heal.'

Danny told him about Chilli and the guy who tried to grab him at Sue's house.

'Best guess, he's about 6'6", bald head, goatee beard and a cauliflower ear. He's bigger than Chilli!'

'He's probably one of Terry Lynch's goons.'

'Lynch? Is he related to Jason Lynch?'

'Terry is Jason's dad. He's also the guy who owns the company that bought your flats, and Chilli works for him.'

The gears in Danny's head clicked and whirred as the pieces of the puzzle came together. He looked at Keith. 'This is not likely to end well, is it?'

***

Danny headed back to the motorway and the hills and valleys of North Wales. Megan was at reception again and looked surprised to see him.

She smiled. 'Can't get enough of our beautiful Welsh air?'

She held out the key to Colin's caravan. He'd left it with her just in case someone else needed it.

'You'll be after this, I presume.'

'Thanks,' he said and reached for the key, but she kept hold of it.

'Password?'

He smiled, and she let go. After dumping his gear, he made a coffee and sat on the bench at the back of the caravan, admiring the view across the fields. It reminded him of a painting above his mum's fireplace. He could have looked at it for hours, but he hadn't come for the view.

***

Chilli phoned Terry, and without preamble, told him what had happened.

'Who is this guy, Chilli?' Terry asked after a long pause. 'Does anyone know anything about him?'

'None of my contacts know him. He wasn't on anyone's radar until he broke Jason's leg and his wife fell off the balcony.'

'That was his wife?'

'Yeh, same night he glassed me in the face.'

There was another long pause. Chilli was tempted to break the silence but kept quiet. It was best to let Terry take as long as he needed to process the information.

'So he's a nobody who's lost his wife, broken my son's leg, and on two separate occasions got away from my two best men without a scratch.'

There was another prolonged silence.

'That doesn't sound like a nobody does it, Chilli. Dig deeper.'

Twenty-Seven

Danny phoned TL Holdings Ltd. He bounced from one recorded message to another like the prize in a pass-the-parcel game until, eventually, the line went dead. His fifth call went through to an answering machine.

'My name is Danny Valik. We need to talk, Mr Lynch. Call me on this number.'

Terry's secretary picked up the message when she got into the office the following day and passed it on to Terry.

On Thursday morning, Danny phoned Sue to ask how she was getting on with the arrangements for Jackie's funeral. She said the coroner wouldn't release Jackie's body until the police investigation was concluded. She told him Detective Inspector Latchford had been in touch and was concerned that Danny hadn't gone to the station for his interview.

'I think he believes you, but he's got to follow procedure. He asked me for your number; I gave it to him. Hope that's okay.'

It wasn't, but Danny let it go. 'I'll call him later.'

Shortly after he'd spoken to Sue, his phone rang – *Private number*. He answered the call and waited for someone to speak.

'Mr Valik.' It was a statement, not a question. 'You wanted to talk to me.'

The voice sounded calm and controlled with a hint of impatience.

'Yes, Terry. We need to sort this out before it gets out of hand.'

'What did you have in mind?'

'You're probably pissed off about what I did to Jason, and I'm sorry about that. I was having a hard time dealing with my wife's cancer, and everything came to a head after she died. It wasn't the cancer that killed her, and Jason didn't kill her, but he was partly to blame for what happened. If he hadn't been trying to force his way into our home, she would still be alive. I was angry, and I made a mistake in the heat of the moment. I'll take whatever punishment the courts see fit to give me.'

Terry laughed. 'Court! This won't be going to court, Danny boy. Your punishment will come from me, and when I'm done, there are other guys lined up who want a chat with you.'

Danny let Terry vent his anger.

Terry continued. 'I must admit, I didn't expect to hear you apologising after your rampage. Glassing people in pubs, breaking bones and killing your wife. You've managed to stay out of everyone's way until now, but not anymore. We'll be getting together pretty soon, you and me. Then we'll see what you're made of.'

Danny took a deep breath. His adrenalin levels and his anger were starting to rise in equal measures. *Not good.*

'Jason's statements about his broken leg and me pushing my wife off the balcony are lies, and I'll fight them to my last breath. The two men who attacked me at my sister's house deserved what they got.'

Terry stayed silent and Danny connected the dots. 'You sent them, didn't you!' He didn't wait for an answer. 'I was defending myself. What would you have done in that situation, Terry?'

There was a pause and then a sigh on the other end of the phone. 'Probably the same as you, Danny boy, but this isn't about me. It's about you hurting my family and making a fool out of me. The Lynch family will not tolerate disrespect.' The line went dead.

***

Sue sat at the dining room table with a cup of tea, recalling recent events. In the last five days, her best friend had died, her brother had been in a bar fight, and two guys had tried to break into her home. It was a lot to take in.

She'd wanted to spend as much time with Jackie as she could before the cancer took its toll, but that wasn't going to happen now. Mike's job paid well enough to ensure that she didn't have to work, so she often took Jackie for her chemotherapy appointments if Danny couldn't make it. Sometimes the three of them went to the hospital together.

Sue wanted to be with Jackie at the end, to hold her hand and comfort her. It was so hard. She couldn't imagine the complex mix of emotions

Danny must be going through. *He wouldn't do all those terrible things under normal circumstances.* She began to cry again.

There was a knock at the door. She wiped her eyes and went to answer it. After what had happened, she was wary of opening the door to anyone. It was a solid UPVC door with a thin frosted glass panel at the top to let in light yet provide privacy, but it also prevented her from seeing who was outside. Mike had talked about putting a peephole in the door, but it was on their 'To-Do' list.

'Who is it?' she asked.

'Police.'

She opened the door and stared into the grinning face of the gorilla. She used all her strength to try and close the door, but his foot was in the way.

He pushed her back into the house and shut the door. 'Just want a chat, Sue. Don't make things difficult.'

***

DI Latchford sipped at his camomile tea and studied the writing on the whiteboard in the corner of his office. DC Richards was chewing the end of his pen.

'Do you believe him, Sir?'

The inspector took another sip.

'The statements from Jason and his mates, along with the bruising on Jackie's arm, the other acts of violence and him fleeing the scene are strong evidence against him.'

'But it's totally out of character. His wife was dying anyway, so why would he throw her off the balcony? And the statements aren't exactly convincing, are they? There are a few anomalies _ '

'Anomawhats?' queried the inspector.

'Differences, Sir, there are a few differences between their statements. And I wouldn't call them reliable witnesses or upstanding citizens, would you? The defence lawyers would have a field day with them.'

The inspector stared into his paper cup.

'We asked him to come in and give us a statement, Steve, and he hasn't. He's the prime suspect in a suspicious death investigation and he's disappeared again.'

The inspector stood resolutely.

'Issue a warrant for his arrest. Put a tag on his phone and get the registration number of his bike. Let's find him.'

Twenty-Eight

Danny's phone rang. It was Sue, which he thought was strange after only speaking to her a little while ago.

'There are two men in the house with me, Danny,' she said, sounding frightened and angry. 'They want to know where you are.'

Danny heard a sharp crack, like a whip. He heard Sue swearing, then a man's voice came on the line.

'I don't make a habit of hitting women, Danny, but she won't tell me where you are.'

It was Chilli. Without thinking, Danny said, 'Does your face hurt? I'll make sure it hurts a lot more if you touch her again.'

There were a few seconds of silence and then came noises that sounded like a scuffle. Sue was swearing, but another sharp crack silenced her. Chilli came back on the phone.

'I can do this all day, Danny. My hand might ache, but ask yourself, what's it doing to her brain? It's not like I have small hands.' He sounded like he was enjoying himself. 'She might end up not looking like your sister anymore, or worse still, she might not recognise you next time she sees you.'

His voice turned into a low growl. 'Where are you?'

The red mist descended in front of Danny's eyes.

'I'll see you soon, Chilli, and when I do, I'm going to hurt you worse than anything you can do to my sister.'

He hung up, dialled the emergency services and gave them Sue's address. To make sure they weren't slow getting there, he added that two men with guns were assaulting a woman in the house.

Danny phoned Keith. 'Tell me where Chilli Edwards hides out.'

Keith heard a calculated coldness in Danny's voice.

'Let the police handle it. You can't mess about with these people, Danny. For a start, there are too many of them. And second, Terry's connections go far and wide.'

'I'll work something out.'

Keith sighed and gave him an address where Chilli had an office in the town centre. It was a couple of rooms above the flower shop on Regent Street.

'There's only one way in and one way out.'

'I owe you, Keith.'

He got on his bike and rode to Runcorn. The police would get to Sue's house before he could, but he needed something to focus on. Chilli wouldn't hang about at Sue's for long if she didn't tell him anything. Danny was guessing he'd probably head to his office.

He parked the bike near a row of red-brick terraced houses under the bridge that crossed the river. He headed for Chilli's office with his rucksack over his shoulder and helmet under his arm, passed the Clarendon where it had all kicked off, and turned right into Regent Street. He passed the flower shop on his right, where he always bought anniversary roses for Jackie, then went up the narrow, one-way street, and passed the kebab shop where they always got something to eat after a Saturday night out. At the top of the street by the traffic lights, he crossed over and slowly strolled back down.

There weren't many people about, which was probably a good thing. Danny looked up at the window above the flower shop. Keith told him if the blinds were open, Chilli was there – they were open. Danny crossed the street and pressed the buzzer next to the white UPVC door.

There was a scratchy click, and Chilli's voice came across the intercom. 'What!'

'Package delivery,' Danny said, trying to disguise his voice by copying how Megan spoke to him in her lilting Welsh accent.

'Put it in the hallway at the bottom of the stairs.'

A buzzer sounded, and the door opened. Danny went in and struggled up the narrow stairs with his rucksack and helmet. At the top of the stairs, a corridor led to two doors on the left. The first door was shut, but the second was open. Chilli was sitting behind a huge desk facing the door, his back to the window overlooking the street. The desk was something to behold and looked like it cost a small fortune. Chilli saw him looking.

'Nice isn't it. Mahogany. We had to take the window out to get it in. Stopped the traffic in the street for three hours.'

Danny walked toward the front of the desk and stood opposite Chilli. 'You're not surprised to see me?'

Chilli grinned, or was it a grimace? It was hard to tell with the cuts on his face.

'I knew hurting your sister would make you look for me, and everyone knows I spend a lot of time here. I guessed it wouldn't take you long to find me, and here you are.' He pointed at a CCTV monitor on the corner of the desk. 'I saw you at the door. You need to work on that accent. It was crap.'

'It wasn't meant to impress.'

He took a step forward and dropped his rucksack on the floor.

'This is going to stop now. Tell Terry Lynch to stay away from my family. And you, if you come anywhere near my sister again, I'll kill you.'

Chilli grunted like a pig at a trough. 'Kill me? Ha! You've been lucky 'til now.'

He leant forward and placed his gorilla arms on the desk. 'I'll call Terry and let him know you're here, and then I'll take you somewhere we can all have a proper chat.'

Grinning like a hyena, he reached for the mobile on the desk.

'No need for that,' Danny said through clenched teeth. 'I'm not hanging around.'

'You're not going anywhere without me,' Chilli said as he put the phone to his ear.

Danny tightened his grip on the chin guard of his helmet and stepped up to the desk. Chilli raised his left hand in a stop gesture, and Danny smashed the helmet down on it. Chilli dropped the phone, grabbed his wrist and stared at Danny. He was expecting another crushing blow, but instead, Danny reached down and pressed the 'end call' button on the phone. Chilli was breathing heavily.

'Full of surprises, aren't you' he snarled.

He reached for the gun taped under his desk, and pointed it at Danny. 'Now sit there while I make this call.'

Danny looked at the Berreta pointed at his heart and smiled. 'I don't think so; the safety's on.'

As Chilli looked at the gun, Danny stepped forward and swung the helmet at Chilli's head. It connected with a thud, and he fell to the floor, unconscious.

Danny knew that motorbike helmets were built to be light but strong. They have to be so they can sit on your head for hours and still do the job of protecting you from injury if you fall. *Impressive, the perfect 'unconcealed' weapon*. He picked up the gun and checked the safety. He'd been wrong. The safety was off, ready to go. Chilli should have known that, but Danny was grateful he didn't. After checking the gorilla was still breathing, he phoned Inspector Latchford. DC Richards answered.

'The inspector isn't here today,' he said. 'He's on annual leave, so his work phone diverts to me.'

'Is my sister alright, Detective?'

'Call me Steve,' he said. 'And yes, she's okay. Whoever assaulted her got away. The officers in the car didn't get the message to keep their siren off.'

'It was a guy called Chilli Edwards,' Danny said. 'He works for Terry Lynch. I spoke to him on the phone while he was at the house. Sue will tell you it was the same guy who tried to knock the door down yesterday.'

'She won't tell us anything, Danny. She's okay like I said, but she's got concussion and a black eye. She's pretty messed up.' Steve waited but continued when danny said nothing.

'It would help if you came to the station for an interview. I can't be certain, but my instincts tell me you didn't kill your wife. Things look bad, but I don't think the evidence we've got will be substantiated in a court of law.'

'What does that mean?'

'Erm, upheld or shown to be true.' He waited again. 'The longer you keep running, the worse it's going to get, Danny. The inspector has already issued a warrant for your arrest.'

Danny ended the call.

A minute or so later, he received a text. *Danny, this is my private mobile. Call me anytime if I can help with anything. Steve.* Steve wanted Danny to trust him, but he had to tread lightly. Getting involved could jeopardise the investigation.

He'd always wanted to be a policeman. He joined up as a constable five years ago after he left school and then decided he wanted to be a detective. The exams were easy, and he'd only been in the post for a short time, but he loved it and wanted to make inspector one day. Working with Harry was an excellent opportunity to learn the ropes.

Harry had been with the Police for over 30 years. Officers often talked about the complexity of murder enquiries and how Harry had solved the notorious case many years ago. Whenever Steve asked Harry what had happened, he changed the subject. He refused to talk about it for some reason, so Steve let it be.

The investigation into Jackie Valik's death was Steve's first case of 'death from suspicious circumstances.' He didn't want to mess it up. He looked into Danny's background and was surprised to find that he'd been an officer in the Territorial Army for about 18 years. He worked in the REME, the Royal Electrical and Mechanical Engineers, and had been posted to Afghanistan on two separate occasions. He'd seen action, but his online file didn't give any specific details. A lot of the paperwork had 'Official Secrets Act' stamped across it. Danny had come home with a medal, and Steve couldn't help but admire him.

***

Chilli woke on the office floor with a banging headache. He got up and quickly sat back down as a moment of dizziness and nausea hit him.

How does that tosser do it? It's not like he's big or scary. It's just so sudden and totally unexpected. I think I'll keep this little adventure to myself. Terry doesn't need to know. Neither does anyone else, for that matter.

Twenty-Nine

Terry couldn't believe what he was hearing.

'—so I slapped her around a bit to see if she would tell me where he was, but she's tough as nails. Someone called the police, and I had to leave.'

Terry waited for a moment before saying 'This habit you've got of letting people slip through your fingers needs sorting out Chilli. Otherwise, we'll have to take a look at your pinkies and find out what the problem is.'

He let that hang in the air between them for a few seconds.

'So, have you found him?'

There was a pause. 'Not yet, boss.'

Terry put the phone down, turned around and began smashing anything he could kick or punch. He messed up the room, destroying chairs, shelves, mirrors and ornaments before he eventually picked up the phone again.

'Chilli,' he said calmly, like a parent talking to a naughty child, 'this guy is making a fool out of all of us, especially me, and I can't have that. It 's not good for business. Just get him. No more phone calls until he' s in your hands. Understand?'

Chilli understood.

***

Sue phoned Mike. She didn't want to, but she had to warn him about her bruised face. Mike was enraged.

'I'm going to kill those arseholes. Who do they think they are —'

'Mike! I'm okay. It's just a few bruises, that's all. It could have been worse.'

'We'll sort these scum out when I get home babe, don't you worry!'

'I know,' she said. 'Will you speak to Danny? He's afraid they may come back here if he's around, so he's gone back to the caravan. Now I'm even more worried about what he'll do.'

'I'll try. I'll be home tomorrow, super early, just in time for breakfast.'

***

Assistant Chief Constable Tustin was having another bad day. Once again, he thought of his retirement next year. It was the only thing keeping him going at the moment. *Thirty-five years as a copper is more than enough for anyone!*

His bosses and the local MP were getting impatient with the Jackie Valik investigation. They wanted results, the case closed and put to bed. It hung over everyone like the clouds of poisonous gas venting into the atmosphere from the chemical works next to the river.

He gazed at the two detectives sitting across the desk from him. Harry Latchford was a good officer. They'd known each other for years and had often spent time together after work unwinding over a couple of drinks. Harry had a good record in cases like this. The youngster sitting next to him was his latest protégé, and apparently, he had potential.

The chief sat back, trying to appear relaxed so the two men in front of him would feel the same.

'So, Harry, where are we up to with the Valik investigation?'

'Well, as you know, Sir, the coroner won't release Jackie's body until we conclude our investigation, and he won't sign anything off until we explain the bruises on her arm. Unfortunately, Danny Valik hasn't given us a formal statement yet, but there's a warrant out for his arrest. We've interviewed Jason Lynch and his two mates and we're looking into their statements.'

Harry took a breath. 'We've also received a complaint from a member of the public who claims that Danny Valik smashed a beer glass into his face at the Clarendon on Church Street on Saturday night.'

'Have you got a statement to that effect?'

'No, Sir. The person who reported the alleged incident made the complaint by phone. He didn't want to make an official statement.'

'Have we got a name and address for this person?'

'No, Sir.'

'Then it's hearsay. Ignore it. What else have you got?'

'Not a lot, to be honest. We've spoken to Danny, but, as I said, he hasn't given us a statement yet.'

The chief leaned forward and shuffled through the paperwork on the desk in front of him.

'I see there's been a request for his phone to be tagged.'

'Yes, Sir. I thought it would be a good way to find out where he's hiding.'

The chief sat back and steepled his hands together in front of him as if he were praying. 'Anything else?'

Harry said, 'There have been two instances of forced entry at the house where Danny's sister lives. We had just left the premises when we received a call to go back. One man had forced his way into the house and attacked Danny. That man sustained injuries during the ensuing struggle, and we were able to arrest him. The accomplice of the injured man tried to break into the house, but we believe he took off when he heard the sirens.'

'Who injured the man, Valik or his sister?'

'We don't know, Sir,' Steve answered.

'Didn't the injured man give you a statement?'

'No, Sir. He didn't want to press charges for the injuries he'd sustained. Danny's sister wouldn't give us a statement either. She just wanted him out of her house.'

The chief frowned. 'Did you get a name and address for the injured man?'

'Yes, we did,' Harry said. 'We checked it out, and the description of the man and the address in Liverpool came back okay. There was nothing we could hold him for.'

The chief's frown turned into a grimace. He leant forward when it became evident that Harry had nothing more to add.

'And?'

Harry held up his hands. 'We had to let him go.'

The chief sat back with a growl. 'And the second incident?'

Harry turned to Steve. 'Can you give the chief the details?'

Steve opened his notebook and found the page he needed.

'Someone dialled the emergency services and reported a disturbance in progress at an address on the Beechwood estate, where Danny's sister Sue Stevens lives. The operator sent a car straight away, and when it arrived, the officers found the front door open and Sue Stevens lying injured in the living room. They checked she was okay and phoned an ambulance. The paramedics treated her for concussion and bruising. She didn't go to hospital and there was no one else at the scene.'

'Thanks, Steve,' the chief said, contemplating his family photograph. He was looking forward to spending more time with them when he retired.

He looked up at his two detectives.

'This sounds like more than a coincidence. Two attacks at the same address within a couple of days. Can we link them?'

Steve consulted his notebook again.

'We know that Danny was at the house when the incident occurred on Wednesday, and we believe that he was the person who made the call to the emergency services about the second incident on Thursday.'

'And Jason Lynch with the broken leg, is he anything to do with Terry Lynch?'

'Yes,' said Harry. 'Jason is Terry's son.'

'Ah,' said the chief, 'I see.'

Thirty

Jason wasn't happy living with his parents again. It was making him irritable. His mum was treating him like a kid, and his dad was – well – his dad was the arsehole he always was. Jason wanted to get back to the flat in Runcorn. Having a place of his own had been liberating and not having to answer to anyone meant he could pretty much do what he liked. Parties with his mates and a few local scrubbers were the highlight of the week – the perks of having a place of his own.

Word was out about the penthouse suite, and all the girls wanted to see it and admire the views. He was happy to let them as long as they were willing to party, which they were most of the time. The town itself was a shit-hole, but having lived amongst the yokels for a little while, he began to see it as an opportunity. Yes, it was Chilli's patch at the moment, but that wouldn't take much to change.

He made his way to the kitchen, trying not to trip on the crutches. They were becoming the bane of his life. He was going to hurt Danny Valik when he got hold of him, despite what his dad had said. He heard his parents arguing. Nothing unusual about that these days. He would have gone back to his room and come back later, but he heard his name mentioned and stopped outside the door to listen.

'I don't know how much longer he'll be here,' Karen said. 'You can see he's not ready to go back to the flat and look after himself yet. Can't you just stay out of each other's way for a little while longer?'

'This is my house.'

'Yes, and he's your son. You can't throw him out. He needs us.'

'He always needs us. He's always been a pain in my backside. Everything has been given to him on a plate, and he doesn't appreciate it.'

'But he's your son and—'

Terry raised his voice. 'I know he's my son, but I don't have to like him. The sooner he goes back to the flat, the better.'

And there it was. His dad had said out loud what he was thinking.

Karen heard the tap of crutches moving along the corridor. She gave Terry a cold stare.

'He must have heard us,' she whispered. 'How could you say that about him?'

She stormed out of the kitchen after her son.

***

It was Thursday afternoon, and Danny was back at the caravan in Llysfaen. He called TL Holdings Ltd. and left a message.

His phone rang; it was Mike.

'How are you, mate?'

Danny began to choke with emotion.

'It's a mess, Mike. I don't know what to do. I'm trying to get hold of this Terry Lynch guy who seems to run everything. I've got the police on my back, and Jackie isn't here anymore.'

'Did you say, Terry Lynch?' Mike asked.

'Yes, why? Do you know him?'

'I knew someone called Terry Lynch a long time ago. He was the last guy I punched without a reason. That Terry Lynch left the factory before me and there were rumours at the time that he'd gotten involved with some unsavoury characters in Liverpool.' Mike was deep in thought, but quickly came back to the present. 'Things might look a bit pear-shaped at the moment mate, but you've been through worse and come out the other side.'

'I know, but Jackie was always there, waiting for me at home. That's what kept me going. Now I can't think straight.'

Mike didn't have any answers for him. After a while, he said, 'I'm on the red-eye flight tomorrow morning, so just let me know if you need anything.'

'Cheers,' Danny said.

He was about to end the call then remembered something. 'I need somewhere to stay. Do you know someone who might be able to rent me a room? All this travelling is doing me in.'

'I'll ask around,' Mike said. 'In the meantime, you might want to think about getting another phone. These latest phones all have GPS in them. The police will be able to find you if they haven't already. Have you got any of your kit with you?'

'No, it's locked in a metal box in the garage.'

'I'll go and take a look tomorrow morning after I've dropped my gear at home and checked on Sue. See if I can get it for you. Have you changed the locks since you gave us the keys?'

'No, the locks are the same. Don't go on your own, Mike. A couple of Jason's mates tried to grab me when I took the bike from the garage, so I presume they're keeping an eye on the place.'

'Don't worry.' said Mike.

***

Danny's phone rang – *Private number.* He answered and waited for someone to speak.

'It seems I underestimated you, Danny boy. You can handle yourself. Your background probably explains how you've managed to evade us, but trust me, that won't happen again.'

Danny remained silent.

'The list of people you've made into enemies just gets longer by the day, doesn't it?'

Danny spoke through gritted teeth.

'It's not my enemies I care about; it's my family and friends. Your fight is with me, not them. You involved my family, and that's not acceptable. I'll show you how that feels, Terry, and then maybe we can come to an understanding.'

'Not acceptable?' shouted Terry down the phone, 'Who do you think—'

Danny disconnected the call.

Terry stared at his phone, smashed it to pieces and threw it on the floor. He couldn't believe that this 'no-mark' was threatening him. He slammed his fists down onto the table in frustration and thought about his next move.

Karen came into the room.

'Can you get me a new phone?' he asked, pointing at the one in bits on the floor. 'Same type, same number, as soon as you can.'

Karen let out a sigh. 'Yes, I'll get you another new phone.'

'And by the way,' she said, 'Jason's gone. He heard what you said and doesn't want to be here anymore. One of his friends came and picked him up.'

Terry nodded but said nothing. After Karen left, he found a glass and poured himself a whisky.

***

As Steve was heading home for dinner, an officer ran up to him with a note. He marched into Harry's office with a smile on his face and the piece of paper held out in front of him.

'We've found him!'

The inspector smiled. He took the piece of paper and looked at the address.

'North Wales off the A55. Excellent.'

'Yes, it's a caravan park,' Steve replied. 'Shall we send a car?'

Harry looked at his watch. 'Have you got much on tonight? Fancy a bit of overtime? I have to write a report for the chief, and then we can head out.'

'Sure, how long will the report take?'

'An hour should do it. The local MP insists on a blow by blow account of events starting with the bar fight on Saturday night. I've got until 8 pm to get it done. Hopefully, we can grab Danny when he's asleep. I want us to bring him in.'

'My mother-in-law is coming for dinner, Sir. Can I quickly pop home to say hello? If I don't, I'll never hear the end of it.'

'Be back by eight,' said Harry

Thirty-One

Before he got into bed, Danny phoned Sue to make sure she was okay and let her know that he would be there around nine tomorrow morning. He let her know that he'd spoken to Mike.

He was worn out but lay awake thinking about his telephone conversation with Terry. Someone was giving Terry information that wasn't available to the general public. *Fingers in pies.* He had to level the playing field. After some thought, he came up with a risky idea he thought might work. He mentally shrugged, accepting the fact that everything he did now would involve some sort of risk but he had to make sure it ended well for him and his family. He sighed. *How has my life come to this?*

He fell into a fitful sleep, full of frustration and despair. He woke without moving. Something had alerted his senses. He blinked his eyes several times to clear his vision, but it was taking too long. He heard the handle on the door opening slowly, then the whisper of a countdown. '3–2–'

He jumped out of bed as the door crashed open and the moonlit silhouette of a man burst in, accompanied by an explosion of light. He put his hands up to shield his eyes, and a blow to the stomach knocked the wind out of him. He dropped to his knees. Two more man-shapes came through the door and stood over him.

'Hello, Danny.'

It was Chilli.

Danny saw something swing towards his head, and he returned to his dreams of frustration and despair.

***

David Bowie was singing 'We could be heroes—' and someone on the radio was talking too quickly about how much was in the pot for this week's prize draw. He guessed he was in the back of a car on a motorway, judging by the speed and number of cars going past. He lay still, his head throbbing. Something sticky clung to the hair on the left side of his head. His hands were tied in front of him, but his legs remained free. A large man sat next to him, Chilli and the driver were in the front. *Three men.* Chilli was taking precautions.

***

Harry and Steve arrived at Mountain View Caravan Park late that night. Harry had only finished his report at 8.15 pm and had insisted on stopping to eat. They spoke to the woman at reception who said she didn't recognise the description of the person they were looking for. They asked if they could have a look around.

Megan shrugged. 'Can't stop you can I.'

'Nice and quiet here, isn't it,' said Steve as they headed for the door.

'It was until ten minutes ago when a car left here spinning its wheels – woke us all up. And now you!'

They walked around the caravan site using their phones as torches and came to caravan number 15. Harry knocked a few times, but there was no answer. They peered through the windows but couldn't see anything. Around the side, they found a red Honda matching the registration of Danny's bike.

Back at reception, Harry asked Megan who owned caravan number 15.

'It belongs to a guy called Colin. He's on holiday in Spain at the moment.'

'Surname?' Steve asked with his notebook and pen in hand.

She gave him a dirty look and reluctantly checked the computer.

'Dean,' she said. 'Colin Dean.'

'Who does the motorbike belong to?' Steve asked.

Megan shrugged. 'It must be Colin's.'

'It's not,' Harry said. 'It belongs to a guy named Danny Valik. Do you know him?' She shook her head and looked away.

Harry sighed and turned to Steve. 'Let's go.'

Steve gave Megan his business card.

'In case you remember something that might help.'

She took the card and dropped it into the recycling bin behind the counter.

***

Chilli took Danny to a derelict social club in Halewood in Liverpool. It was situated at the edge of a ten-year-old housing estate and backed onto a wood. The owners had run into financial difficulties and closed it down. The building was due to be demolished soon to make way for more new houses.

The security guard employed to keep an eye on the site gave Terry the keys for the building in exchange for an envelope full of cash. It helped feed his four kids and pay his rent. Terry knew money could convince good people to do things they wouldn't normally do. One of his contacts at the council told him it would be a few months before the demolition company came to knock the place down. Until then, he was going to make the most of it. It was the perfect location for Chilli to have a quiet chat with Danny.

After dragging him in from the car, they tied him to a wooden chair next to a table.

'I need the toilet,' said Danny.

'Go ahead,' said Chilli.

Danny took a piss in his pants, ignoring the look of disgust on their faces. The relief it brought was worth it, but he had a feeling it wasn't going to last.

Thirty-Two

Ryan's arm itched like mad when he woke on Friday morning. The cast wasn't due to be taken off for a while, but he longed for a proper shower, the feeling of being clean and smelling clean. He'd asked his mum and sister for help, but they were useless. They let water get between his arm and the cast, and when he said it had to stay dry, they told him to do it himself as he was so ungrateful.

After experimenting, he found the best way to keep it dry was to put his whole arm in a bin bag and tape it up at the shoulder. It worked well, but taping the bag with one arm was difficult and usually took longer than the shower.

His mum and sister moaned and whined about him being useless. It was hurtful because he had always tried his best for them. In the middle of one of their rants, he smiled and remembered how he used to moan and whinge all the time like them. The memory of his childlike behaviour at the hospital when he met Dr Coulton made him cringe.

His phone rang. *'Number withheld'* appeared on the screen. He answered it anyway.

It was Jason Lynch. 'Hey, Ryan, how's things? How's your arm?'

'Hi, Jason. My arm's okay, thanks. The cast is coming off in—'

'Yeh, that's great, mate. Where were you yesterday? I was looking for you. I need some charlie. How soon can you get it here?'

Ryan had spent a lot of time thinking about this scenario. He'd ignored Jason's call the day before, but sooner or later, someone would ask him to deliver drugs, and he would have to deal with it.

'I don't do that anymore. Get someone else to do it.'

'What you talkin' about!' exclaimed Jason. 'You havin' a laugh? Just get the stuff. I'll throw in a few extra quid for your trouble, okay?'

'Nah, it's not the money. I just don't want to do it anymore.'

There was a pause, and Jason lowered his voice. 'Now listen, you little—'

Ryan ended the call and started shaking uncontrollably. He took a few deep breaths and dropped his shoulders, making a conscious effort to get the shaking under control. The conversation had gone to plan. It had been hard, but he'd taken a big step away from the person he used to be.

His sister had been listening. 'Did you just say you're not getting drugs for anyone anymore? You can't do that! I need it!'

Ryan shrugged. 'Not my problem.'

'Mum! Ryan's said he's not getting drugs anynore!'

His mum rushed into the room. 'What! Now listen Ryan_'

'No mum. You listen. I won't be getting any more drugs for anyone and I'm not going to steal again. I'm going to change my life and this is the start.'

She laughed nervously, understanding the far reaching consequences of his acions. 'Don't be stupid. What are you going to do for money? What about me and your sister? You can't change who you are Ryan. You just can't.' she said desperately.

'Watch me' he said.

***

They left Danny sitting in his piss soaked jeans for hours. When they returned, Chilli began pacing back and forth in front of him like a caged tiger.

'I've got a message for you. Somethin' so everybody knows that you can't get away with hurting Mr Lynch's family. I'm sure you understand.'

He stopped pacing and stared into Danny's eyes.

'Breakin' your leg will send out that message.'

He continued his pacing. 'Terry will be here later to have a word, but before that, me and you have unfinished business.'

He put his hand up to the side of his face and gently stroked the cuts that were still healing.

'Every morning, when I look in the mirror, I see the mess you made of my face. I don't look like me anymore! What I see reminds me of you, and I don't want to be reminded of you, Danny.'

'So get rid of the mirror,' said Danny with a grin.

Chilli sighed and shook his head. 'That might work, but there's a lot of mirrors in the world. I couldn't get rid of them all. I would be happier knowing that something I did to you would remind you of me every day.'

Danny grinned. 'You need to slow down cowboy. That's very touching, but your mates here will think something is going on between us.' Danny winked at the two goons standing behind Chilli.

They looked at each other and frowned. 'What's he talkin' about?' the blonde asked.

Chilli stared at them and shook his head. He turned back to Danny and smiled.

'So here's what we're going to do.'

He removed a cloth that covered a silver tray on the table. There was a knife, a blow torch, a bottle of cheap vodka and some bandages.

'Before we break your leg, I'm goin' to cut off the little finger on your left hand.'

Danny began to fidget, testing the ties around his wrists.

'And just so you don't forget this experience, I'm doin' it one joint at a time.'

He stopped pacing and stood directly in front of Danny.

'Three cuts until it's gone completely. I think that'll remind you of me every day and make things even between us.'

Danny stared into his eyes.

'It won't make things even for me.'

Chilli laughed. 'You want to make some more stupid comments about what's goin' on between us, or shall we just get started?'

He nodded at his men. As they grabbed hold of him, Danny's heartbeat began ramping up like a steam train trying to reach top speed. The two men cut the cable tie that bound his hands and tied his right arm to the side of the chair. Danny struggled but couldn't stop what was happening. One of the men went behind him and put an arm around his throat in a chokehold.

The blonde attempted to tie Danny's left hand to the table. Danny made a fist and was trying hard not to let him. The 'choker' behind him increased the pressure on his throat, and Danny passed out. He woke up when Chilli slapped him in the face. Danny saw that his wrist was now cable tied to the table, and the blonde was holding his left hand down with the little finger exposed. Chilli fired up the blow torch and put the knife into the flame.

'It helps the blade slice through the tendons,' he said matter of factly, 'and cauterises the wound.'

Danny tried to free himself, but the chokehold and the grip on his hand were too tight. The thought of blacking out again and missing what was happening to his finger sounded like a good option. He wanted to turn away, but couldn't move his head or do anything as Chilli moved the knife towards his finger. He screwed his eyes shut and held his breath. He felt the heat on his finger and opened his eyes. The tip of his little finger lay about an inch away from his hand. He wanted to scream but clenched his jaw and stayed silent as Chilli poured some vodka onto the bloody stump and tightly wrapped a bandage around it.

'We don't want you bleedin' all over our table, do we Danny,' he smirked.

He put the knife back into the flame just as the door burst open.

Thirty-Three

Sue and Jackie were best friends and were delighted when Danny and Mike became brothers-in-law, and eventually, best friends. They all got on well together and often went out as a foursome. Mike had spent many Saturdays working on Jackie's car or Danny's bike in their rented garage at the flats. Afterwards, they would go to the Clarendon as a reward for their hard work, and the girls would join them later on. Sometimes the boys went out on their own, usually to the Clarendon on a Saturday afternoon to watch the match and put the world to rights.

They both had an interest in anything to do with the Army. Danny was always buzzing when he returned home from his weekends away with the Territorial Army. Mike loved hearing his stories. He had wanted to join the Army but had never enlisted for one reason or another. After seeing how much Danny enjoyed the TA, Mike signed up, and their bond became stronger. Danny didn't need to ask Mike for help when he was in trouble.

***

Mike got out of his car and unlocked the garage. Danny's kit was hidden in a large, metal toolbox chained to the back wall. He removed the old, grey army blanket, unlocked the box, took out the battered sports bag inside and slung it over his shoulder. When he closed the garage door, he was aware of someone behind him

'Hey, mate.'

Two lads in their early twenties stood in front of him nervously passing a joint between them. One of them wore a dark blue sports top with the hood up over his head. His mate was taller and wore a black leather biker jacket.

'What you doin' ?' hoody asked.

Mike ignored him and walked towards his car. Leather jacket stepped in front of him. He was about the same height as Mike but not as well built.

'That's my mate's garage,' hoody said. 'What you got in the bag?'

Mike sighed. 'It's not your mate's garage, it's my mate's garage. Go and play somewhere else before you get hurt.'

Mike shouldered leather jacket out of his way and walked towards the car.

'Hey tosser!' hoody exclaimed, throwing the joint to the ground as they both made a move towards him. The sound of a car horn distracted them, and the three of them watched as two men squeezed out of Mike's car. Mike's brothers were younger and bigger than him. They unmercifully took the mickey out of him for only being 6'2" and the runt of the men in the family.

John walked over and stood next to Mike. Hoody's eye began to twitch as Johns 6' 5" frame stared down at him.

'Is everything alright?' John asked without shifting his gaze.

'No problem,' said Mike. 'Let's go.'

Thirty-Four

Gary Lynch oozed charisma, that certain something that couldn't be put into words but drew you to him like a magnet. Men wanted to be his friend, women wanted to bed him. He had presence, strength and a streak of ruthlessness that put Terry in the shade. His brother, however, was way ahead of him in the thinking department and was the reason why he was the Boss.

Terry walked into the old social club and took a good look around. He was wearing his favourite dark blue, fitted suit over a light blue open-necked shirt. Dark brown, leather shoes finished the look. Two of his men stood behind him with their hands clasped in front of them. Gary nodded at the two guys holding Danny, who cautiously nodded back. He strolled forward and stood in front of Chilli, making a point of taking a good look at the cuts on his face.

'It's been a while, Chilli.'

Chilli nodded.

Chilli hadn't seen or talked with Gary since the Sophie incident and never understood why Gary didn't exact revenge for his betrayal. The tension between them was electric, like two storm clouds headed towards one another, ready to explode.

Gary turned his attention to Danny.

'So this is the guy Terry's been looking for. He doesn't look like he could cause so much trouble.'

He walked around the table and saw the bandaged hand and severed fingertip

He faced Danny and said 'Unlike my brother, I won't underestimate you.'

He winked and turned around to face Chilli.

'Untie him.'

'I can't do that, Gary. Terry—'

'Terry isn't here!' screamed Gary.

Chilli flinched. The two men holding Danny took a step back. Gary's temper was well known. There was evidence that it was worse than his brother's, but there weren't many people left to ask about it. Gary turned and nodded to his men. They both took guns out of their pockets and pointed them at Chilli and his men.

Gary stared at Chilli. 'You know I never ask twice!'

Chilli hesitated for a microsecond and nodded at his men. They cut the cable ties and helped Danny to his feet.

Gary smiled at Chilli. 'Good.'

Danny stood unsteadily and walked past Chilli.

'We've got unfinished business,' Chilli said.

Danny held up his bandaged hand in front of him. 'Yes, we have.'

Gary turned and walked towards the door. 'Come with me.'

In the car, one man sat in the front passenger seat with a gun resting on his knee. Danny got in the back next to another man and wasn't surprised to see a gun being pointed at his stomach.

As Gary drove off, he sniffed loudly. 'Jeez, what's that smell?'

He opened the windows.

'I took a piss,' said Danny.

Gary nodded. 'Understandable in the circumstances.'

'Before he cut me.'

Gary smiled and looked in the rear-view mirror. *I could get to like you, Danny. You've got balls.*

'Sorry to hear about your wife.'

Danny said nothing. He took the bandage away from his finger and had a look at the stump. It wasn't as bad as it could have been. The blade had been sharp, and the cut was clean. Cauterising it meant there was minimal chance of infection. Maybe he should have brought the dismembered fingertip with him. He started to shiver.

Gary noticed. 'Put your coat over him, Tony. Keep him warm.'

He looked at Danny in the mirror again. 'I'll take you to someone who can sort that out for you. Then I'll drop you wherever you want. Okay?'

Danny nodded.

'Why are you doing this? You don't know me.'

'As long as you're running around making a fool of my brother, he'll do everything he can to find you. He'll use all his resources, and his temper will go into overdrive, and while all that is going on, I'll be sorting a few things out in the background.'

Danny looked out of the window for a second or two. 'I'm a distraction.'

Gary smiled

Gary's doctor was getting on a bit but seemed to be doing a good job of sorting out Danny's finger.

'Could you have stitched the tip back on if I'd brought it with me?' Danny asked.

The doctor shook his head. 'There are too many nerves to connect. It would probably have become a hindrance to you over time. You're better off without it.' He gave Danny a large bag of antibiotics and painkillers. 'Take them; they'll help.'

Gary passed the doctor a wad of cash and thanked him for his time.

He turned to Danny. 'Where do you want to go?'

'Anywhere near the Beechwood estate in Runcorn would be fine.'

Gary made a phone call, and they waited for a car to arrive.

'Things are going to change in Terry's world, and it wouldn't be good for you to get caught up in it. Leave your unfinished business with Chilli and Terry until the dust settles.'

Danny shrugged his shoulders. 'I don't know if I can do that.'

'I had a feeling you might say that. If you can't wait, keep out of my way, and we shouldn't have a problem. Understand?'

Danny nodded.

'I don't know if you listen to advice,' Gary said, 'but here's a freebie for you. Don't trust anyone, not even me.'

He drove away as Danny's car arrived.

Thirty-Five

Danny walked through the door at Sue's house wearing the jogging pants and t-shirt he'd had on in bed the previous night.

Sue frowned. 'We were expecting you earlier. Where's your bike?'

Mike noticed the bandage on Danny's finger. 'What happened?'

'Before I tell you, can I have a drink, something to eat and some clothes?'

Sue hugged him and wouldn't let go for a long time. She pulled away from wrinkling her nose. 'I think you could do with a wash as well.'

While he showered, Sue made toast and cups of tea and Mike sorted out some clean clothes. They sat together in the dining room, and inbetween the food and drink, Danny told them what had happened. When he'd finished, Sue hugged him again.

'I got your kit,' Mike said when she let go of him.

'Any problems?' Danny asked.

'Nah, a couple of dicks asking questions, but John and Ray were with me, so no problem.'

They were quiet for a while, each of them lost in thought. Mike broke the silence.

'What do you want to do?'

Danny held his left hand up with the bandaged finger.

'I can't let this go, and what they did to Sue crossed a line.'

Mike and Sue nodded in unison.

Danny stared at the tabletop. 'And Jackie ... she shouldn't have died like that.'

He took a moment to stem the tidal wave of grief that was threatening to overcome him.

'I need to clear my name, otherwise I'm going to prison, and Terry Lynch needs to understand that he can't push people around just because he feels like it. So here's what I'm thinking.'

***

Ryan was starting to feel better about himself. People he'd known for years noticed his newfound confidence and were surprised at how much taller he'd gotten since they last saw him. His mum and sister hardly recognised this new man living in their house. He took ages in the bathroom, the washing machine was on a lot more, and his room smelt fresh.

He thought about moving away and starting over, maybe down south, towards Brighton. Someone had told him it was warmer in that part of the country, but he wouldn't be going anywhere just yet. .

Ryan felt the need to apologise to Alice Lynch, Terry's mum. He wanted to ask forgiveness for knocking her over. Although he'd already been punished and didn't have to, it was the right thing to do. He got a friend to find out where she lived and went to see her.

An old lady with a Zimmer frame eventually came to the door when he knocked. He sheepishly introduced himself to her as the thief who had knocked her over. She put her hand to her mouth.

'I haven't got any money; please leave me alone.'

'I've come to apologise. Can I talk to you for a minute?'

She looked him over. 'Apologise?'

She noticed the cast on his arm. 'What happened?'

Ryan took a moment to think about his answer. *I wonder if she knows what her son is capable of? Should I tell her that Terry broke my arm as punishment for knocking her over?*

'I promise I'm not here to steal from you. I'd just like to talk.'

***

Jason enjoyed being back in the flat. He didn't need his mum, dad, or anyone else to look after him. Food, drink and a bit of dope delivered straight to his door were enough. He ordered some food and drink and called Baz and Neil to come over and party.

He was surprised when Ryan had knocked him back on the drug delivery. He'd just been to a physiotherapy session and wasn't feeling great and decided he needed something to take the edge off. He'd phoned Ryan, and after their short conversation had phoned someone else he knew who delivered his fix. There were plenty of other drug runners out there desperate for cash. Ryan had subsequently been removed from the list of contacts on his phone.

His good mood was shot to pieces when Baz told him that someone had been into Danny's garage and taken a sports bag.

'What was in the bag?' he asked.

'Don't know, Jase.'

'Who was the guy?'

'Don't know, Jase.'

Jason sighed. 'Let's try this another way. What do you know about what happened, Baz?'

Baz held his chin and looked at the ceiling.

'They drove off in a silver Audi!' He clapped his hands in delight.

'Great! What was the registration?'

'Don't know, Jase.'

Baz hung his head in abject failure.

Baz and Neil weren't the brightest flames in the fire, but they were mates, and he would need them when he eventually found Danny.

***

Terry went ballistic when he found out Ryan had visited his mum. She phoned him and told him what a nice boy Ryan was, coming round and apologising for knocking her over.

'He told me you broke his arm. Is that true, Terry?'

'Believe me, Mum,' he said indignantly, 'I didn't break his arm.'

'I believe you, Terry, but I know you better than that. You might not have broken his arm, but you told someone else to do it, didn't you?'

'Mum, I—'

'Why would you do that? It was an accident. He didn't knock me over on purpose. There was no need to hurt him, the poor lad.'

He didn't know what to say. Mothers have a way of making their children feel small, even children as scary as Terry Lynch.

'I've got to go,' she said. 'The Ladies are coming round for a cuppa and a chat in a minute. I'm going to put the kettle on and get the biscuits out. Love you.'

'Love you too, mum.'

And that was it. There was nothing more to be said. She would be fine next time they spoke, but there was no getting away from the fact that she had just put him in his place. The last thing he needed was Ryan and his mum telling everyone that he went around breaking people's arms. *Ryan had better not become a thorn in my side.*

Thirty-Six

Mike offered to collect Danny's stuff from Llysfaen. He would take John with him to bring the bike back. All they needed was the key to the caravan. Danny told him about Megan and Sheba.

'We should only be a couple of hours, depending on the traffic. What are you going to do?'

'I want to go back to the flat and get some clothes and things,' Danny said. 'Things that meant something to me and Jackie. I'll get the keys for the car while I'm there as well.'

Mike frowned. 'Why don't you wait until me and John get back, and we'll come with you.'

'Thanks, Mike, but I need to go on my own. I'll be careful.'

Mike trusted Danny's judgement so left him to it and phoned John to make arrangements to go to North Wales.

Sue offered to drive Danny to the flat, but he felt like walking. It gave him time to prepare for the emotional roller coaster he was about to ride. Jason and his mates might be hanging around, but if he took his time, there shouldn't be a problem. Being alone in the flat with his memories would be more of a challenge.

He walked past the church onto the promenade with the bridge on his left. The flats were ahead on his right, as imposing as ever. An elderly couple sat on a bench, feeding the swans and ducks. A young guy was sitting at another bench, staring at the water. As Danny passed him, he noticed the cast on his left arm and thought he looked familiar. *No time to stop.* He walked on, taking a shortcut that avoided the garages and any surprises that might be lurking in the shadows. He made his way up the emergency stairs at the back of the block and before long, his legs and his lungs began complaining.

He arrived at flat 9a, sucking in air like it was going out of fashion. *I took these stairs two at a time not so long ago!* He waited for his breathing to return to normal and looked at the solid wooden door with the brushed aluminium handle – tarnished from years of use. He used Sue's spare key to get in and closed the door behind him. He stood still, closed his eyes and took a deep breath. Familiar smells and the memories they invoked threatened to open the flood gates to his emotions. He exhaled and took another deep breath when his lungs complained about the lack of oxygen.

Everything about the place reminded him of Jackie. He went into the bedroom to gather some clothes. He left Jackie's stuff, everything except the white t-shirt she wore to bed. He held it to his face and inhaled her perfume, then put it into the holdall he'd brought with him. The car keys were in a kitchen drawer with other important stuff like car and bike ownership papers, insurance policies, bank statements, spare keys, bills, and passports. He pulled the drawer out of the unit and emptied the contents into the holdall.

He didn't have room for all his cherished LPs and CDs, so he picked a few CD's that he couldn't do without, including the first Led Zeppelin album. He could replace the rest over time. He picked up the bronze mouse off the shelf in the bedroom that they'd bought on their honeymoon in Șantorini. That could never be replaced. It wasn't worth much, but the sentimental value was off the scale. He put it in his pocket.

He gently closed the door behind him and went to get Jackie's car. The guy with the cast on his arm was at the bottom of the stairs.

'Hi,' he said, 'can we talk?'

'I'm in a hurry,' Danny said, marching towards the car.

The tall, neatly dressed guy walked alongside him. Danny stopped at the car and turned to face him, trying to remember where he'd seen him before.

'Do I know you?'

'I think so,' he said sheepishly. 'You tripped me when I took that woman's handbag in the high street a few weeks ago?'

Danny recognised him now. 'Yes, that was me. What do you want?'

Danny saw two men walking towards them. They were the males who had been at the flat with Jason and had tried to push him off his bike the night Jackie died. Both were wearing the same clothes they had on that night.

Ryan saw them too. 'Shit,' he muttered under his breath.

Danny ignored them and put the holdall on the back seat of the car. As he opened the front door, the guy in the leather jacket closed it. He grinned at Danny, full of misplaced attitude.

'Hey, Ryan,' said the smaller guy wearing a hoody. 'Long time no see.'

Ryan tried hard not to look away or drop his eyes.

'Hi, Baz.'

Ryan usually looked down at his feet when he spoke to people and Baz had never really seen his face before. For some reason, seeing Ryans steely blue eyes unnerved him. He did a double-take and then turned to Danny.

In his best gangster voice he said 'Jason wants a word with you.'

'I bet he does,' said Danny. 'I've got a few things I want to say to him too, but not today, Baz.'

Danny tried to open the door, but leather jacket kept hold of it and wouldn't let go.

'No, you don't understand,' said Baz. 'We're goin' to see him now.'

Baz nodded at Neil, who grabbed hold of Danny's right arm. Danny opened the door and gave it a short, sharp push that connected with Neil's chest. It knocked the breath out of him, and he doubled over. Danny used his left elbow to rattle Neil's conveniently placed jaw. Neil crashed to the ground like a felled tree. Baz stepped towards Danny, reaching for the knife he kept in his pocket. Ryan stepped in between them. The unexpected behaviour stopped Baz mid-stride, his hand still in his pocket.

Baz looked up at Ryan, not sure what was happening. 'Get out of the way.'

Ryan didn't move. Danny stepped forward and stood next to Ryan.

'Like I said, Baz, not today. Best you sort your mate out, then go and give Jason the bad news.'

Danny turned to Ryan. 'You'd better come with me. Get in the car.'

They drove back up Greenway Road, away from the town centre. Ryan had to crouch down in the seat to avoid banging his head on the roof. Instead of going to Sue's house, Danny went past the Cenotaph at the right hand bend at the top of the road and turned left up the single track lane that led to the hill overlooking the river. Where Ryan went every day. He stopped on a piece of land next to a derelict pub. They sat in silence for a while, and then Danny introduced himself.

'And you must be Ryan,' he said.

Ryan stared out of the window. 'I've never done anything like that before, I think I'm going to be in a shitload of trouble.'

'All you did was stand in his way,' Danny said. 'No big deal.'

Ryan sighed heavily. 'It is to them.'

'How do you feel?'

'A bit sick.'

Danny grinned. 'You did okay. Thanks for stepping in, but I had it covered.'

Ryan smiled. 'Yeh, I think you did, but it was something I had to do for myself.'

He turned to look at Danny.

'Was it your wife's handbag I grabbed outside the supermarket?'

Danny stared straight ahead.

'Yes, it was.'

'Can you tell her I'm sorry for what I did?'

Danny shook his head. 'No, I can't. She's dead.'

Ryan couldn't think of anything to say that would be meaningful. He hadn't known Jackie, and he didn't know Danny, so there was no common ground, no frame of reference he could use to say something appropriate.

'Sorry' he said. He wound his window down, and they sat in mutual silence for a little while longer.

Thirty-Seven

Ryan walked home, and Danny drove to Sue's house. He parked around the corner and walked along the street. Nothing seemed unusual. No one was trying to look inconspicuous. *That's good*. Danny knocked and noticed a new peephole in the door.

Sue opened up and smiled at him. 'You okay? Just making a cuppa.'

He walked into the living room and saw Mike and John on the sofa.

'Any problems?' he asked.

'Nah,' Mike said. 'I've put your phone on charge, and your bike's in John's garage.'

Danny nodded at John.

'Cheers, both of you.'

Sue came in with cups of tea. 'And before I forget, have you been taking your Warfarin tablets, Danny?'

'Sort of,' he replied. 'When I remember.'

Sue scolded him. 'You know you have to take them every day. Make sure you remember.'

'Yes, Mother,' he said with a grin.

'So, how did it go at the flat?' Mike asked.

'It was interesting. I got what I wanted and more besides.'

He proceeded to tell them about Baz and Neil. Mike laughed and said it sounded like the same two idiots he'd met at the garage.

Danny then told them about Ryan. 'He seems like a good guy, just a bit mixed up at the moment.'

Sue was surprised. 'But isn't he the one who snatched Jackie's bag?'

'He asked me to apologise to Jackie. It sounds like he wants to move on from all of that, and I, for one, am happy to help him' said Danny. 'He deserves a second chance.'

Mike smiled. 'You're just feeling guilty about knocking the shit out of him outside the supermarket.'

Danny laughed. 'Maybe, but he wants to turn his life around. Let's see how he gets on.'

***

As part of his plan to get Chilli working for him instead of his dad, Jason phoned Chilli and told him what had happened when his mates confronted Danny and Ryan.

Chilli was surprised. 'Why the hell did Ryan get involved? He's a wimp. Breaking his arm was supposed to send a message. He's clearly too stupid to get it. If he gets in the way again, let me know and I'll break his other arm.'

Jason was delighted. Chilli was unwittingly working for him now. 'I mentioned to my dad that I was gonna get in touch with you and we would be working together, but he doesn't want to be bothered with the details.'

'Typical of Terry,' muttered Chilli. 'Not interested in the small stuff – just get on with it!'

***

Danny went over his plan, and Sue was first to speak. 'You can't be serious! That's kidnapping. For goodness sake, you could all go to jail.'

'I know how it sounds,' said Danny, 'but it's just a way of letting him know he's vulnerable. And he was the one who sent his goons here. That was out of order. If I'm reading it right, Terry won't want to involve the police, so I won't be going to jail – not for that anyway. Assaulting Chilli and Jason will have consequences, but I don't know what they will be yet.'

Mike had his head down, staring at the carpet while Danny talked.

'I think we can make it work, ' he said, 'but I don't know if Terry is the sort of guy who will back off afterwards. And if he doesn't—'

'I know,' said Danny 'but I can't just leave it, otherwise this,' – he said holding up his left hand – 'will remind me every day that I let someone take something from me, and I did nothing about it. No, I've got to do something.'

Mike nodded. 'I understand that. And I'll help.'

John looked at Mike and then at Danny and nodded to both of them.

Sue stood up. 'It doesn't matter what I say, does it. You're going ahead with it anyway, aren't you.'

The three of them nodded.

She shook her head and laughed. 'So what's next for the Three Musketeers?'

'More like the Three Stooges,' said Mike.

***

It didn't take much detective work for Steve to realise that the inspector was becoming more and more agitated the longer the investigation went on. Failing to arrest Danny at the caravan park the previous evening didn't help. They had hung around for a couple of hours to see if Danny would turn up, but he didn't, so they headed home, tired and empty-handed. The update to the chief hadn't gone well, and the higher-ups were running out of patience. They would have been off the case if anyone but Harry had been in charge. They needed results. Steve sent a frustrated text to Danny, advising him to go to the station for his interview.

***

Danny checked his text messages. Colin asked how he was getting on and if Jackie's funeral had been arranged. Danny texted him back straight away, explaining that the police were still looking into her death. He left it at that, knowing Colin would phone him for a chat sooner or later.

He also had a text from Steve, letting him know that they'd been to the caravan looking for him and he should come to the station and sort things out.

The last text was from Ryan, which just said 'hi'. They'd swapped numbers after their chat in the car. Ryan wanted something from him, forgiveness maybe, but Danny didn't know what for. They'd spoken about his broken arm, and Danny showed Ryan his finger. Before they parted, they shook hands and agreed to keep in touch.

Thirty-Eight

Jason had been back at his flat for over a week now but still hadn't bothered to phone his mum. Karen was missing him and decided she needed cheering up. She knew the best way to do that was to go shopping. She loved any kind of shopping, but shopping for clothes was her favourite way to spend Terry's money. All the stores knew that when Mrs Lynch shopped, their profits soared, so they treated her accordingly and indulged her every whim.

Shopping with a friend was even better. It gave them time to catch up on any gossip and complain about the men in their lives.

Karen and her mate Natalie were in the city centre having a great time. They'd started early as usual and by lunchtime were loaded down with designer bags full of clothes and shoes. Karen had made a reservation at one of their favourite, high-end restaurants, so they headed back to the car to dump the bags.

Today she was driving the all-singing, all-dancing Portofino Blue TDV8 Westminster Edition Range Rover that Terry had bought at the Paris Motor Show in 2012. He told her he was taking her away for a romantic weekend, but it was just an excuse for him to be there for the unveiling of the latest edition of his favourite vehicle. As soon as he saw it, he had to have one and put down a deposit.

Terry didn't like his cars getting scratched, so she'd parked in an expensive underground car park that had big spaces and a security guard at the exit barrier. It was worth paying extra to ensure it didn't get scratched or scuffed. Even though it was no longer his favourite Range Rover, it was still the car he used the most, and he would always check the bodywork before going out in it. She didn't want to deal with another of his rants if she took it home damaged. His angry outbursts were getting more intense and more frequent the older he got, and she had become tired of them.

They put their bags in the boot and, arm in arm, headed in the direction of the exit. A man stepped out from behind one of the grey, concrete pillars and stood in front of them. He was wearing a scruffy leather biker jacket that definitely wasn't a fashion statement.

'Karen,' he said, 'I need you to come with me.'

She squeezed Natalie's arm. 'I don't think so.'

They walked around him and carried on towards the exit as another man stepped out of the shadows and blocked their way.

'Terry knows I'm here,' the biker said. 'We should get in the car.'

'Terry sent you?' she asked. 'I haven't seen you before, and I know everyone who works for him.'

'We're associates,' he said. 'Get in the car, and I'll explain.'

'In that case, you won't mind if I call him to find out what's going on,' Karen said as she pushed the speed dial on her phone. The biker snatched it off her and gave it to his mate.

'No calls. Not yet.'

'How do I know you're not going to hurt us?'

'Believe me; I won't.'

'Why should I believe you?'

'Why would I lie? I could have killed you both and walked away before either of you hit the ground. I won't hurt you,' he said gently.

She didn't know why but his deep, brown eyes compelled her to believe him.

She unlocked the car, and the second man took the keys off her.

The biker held the back door open like a proper gentleman and motioned her to get in. He told Natalie to go home as this didn't concern her. She was about to protest when Karen stopped her. 'It's okay, Nat. Just let Terry know.'

The biker got in the back with her, and they drove out.

The security guard in the kiosk didn't even look up from his newspaper. *I won't be parking here again.*

They headed out of the city along Edge Lane and onto the M62.

'Where are we going?' she asked as they drove past the turn off for Huyton.

'Halewood,' said Danny.

Karen looked at him properly for the first time.

'You don't work for Terry, do you. He won't be happy about this, and if you know anything about him, you know you're in deep shit. I wouldn't want to be in your shoes.'

Danny shrugged. 'I've tried speaking to him, but he doesn't want to listen. I'm going to send him a message that'll make him listen. Doing it this way ensures that no one else gets hurt.'

She sighed. 'I don't know what's going on, but this won't solve anything; I'll tell you that for nothing. He'll come after you with everything he's got and hurt you more than you can imagine.'

Danny looked out of the side window. 'I don't think so,' he said quietly.

Mike drove past the abandoned social club, checked around and parked at the side of the building. He listened to the V8 engine tick over for a few seconds, then turned it off.

In the silence that followed, Karen took a closer look at her abductors. She could tell they weren't local hoods aiming to hurt her or hold her to ransom. Then again, local hoods would know it was a bad idea to mess with Terry Lynch. They didn't seem nervous, just efficient. The biker seemed distracted, like he was in another time, or another place, and there was a profound sadness in his eyes when he looked at her.

'Are you going to tell me what's going on?' she asked. 'Natalie will have phoned Terry by now. It won't be long before he finds you. You should go while you can.'

'The manufacturers put GPS trackers in expensive cars like this but we should be okay for about an hour. My name's Danny, by the way, and this is Mike.'

'I would say 'pleased to meet you, Danny,' but I'm not, so I won't. What the hell are you playing at? You're in so much shit—'

'I'm the guy who broke Jason's leg.'

He just about got his arm up in time to block the punch headed towards his face. He grabbed her other arm.

'Who do you think you are!' She shouted at him. 'He wasn't doing anything wrong, and you decided it was okay to break his leg? I hope Terry gets hold of you and does the same to you! See how you like it!'

She continued to struggle, but Danny had a firm grip on her.

'I'll explain what happened if you give me a chance.'

She stopped and stared into his eyes, not sure what to do next. She let her body relax, and he slowly let go of her arms. She listened as he told her about Jackie's cancer and her fall from the balcony. When he talked about Jason, she had to bite her tongue to stop herself from shouting at him again.

She let him continue without interruption, and he told her about the calls to Terry.

He held up his bandaged finger. 'A couple of days ago, I was here, inside this club.'

'I'm sorry about your wife,' she said, 'but Terry wouldn't cut you. He doesn't do that sort of thing.'

'Chilli did it!'

She visibly tensed. 'That's someone you don't want bearing a grudge against you.'

Danny nodded in agreement and noticed the silver Audi pulling into the car park.

Karen noticed too. 'Looks like you're out of time,' she said.

Mike nodded at Danny in the rear-view mirror.

'Listen, I was happy to let the police handle what I did to Jason, but Terry crossed the line when he sent Chilli to play rough with my sister.'

She looked surprised.

'This is just a message, Karen. One I hope he understands. Tell him to stop now and leave me and my family alone.'

Karen looked at him. 'Or what.'

'There's no 'or what' Karen. Just tell him. You can get out now.' Mike returned her phone, and Danny got in the front. They drove away with the Audi following them.

She phoned Terry and told him where she was.

Thirty-Nine

They drove to Widnes and parked in front of a disused warehouse at an abandoned retail park. Sometimes, model car enthusiasts met there on a Sunday morning to race their machines against like-minded fanatics. There was no one around at the moment. No lights, no cameras and no action.

Danny got out of the car and locked it. As he placed the key on the passenger side front tyre, Mike attached a small, black, magnetic disc to the inside of the front bumper bracket. John was waiting for them in the Audi.

'How was it?' he asked. 'Any trouble?'

'No, no trouble,' Danny said. 'Thanks for picking us up.'

Mike handed Danny a piece of paper with a mobile phone number on it. Danny texted the number Mike had retrieved from Karen's phone.

'I'd have thrown the keys away, made it difficult for him,' Mike said.

'That Range Rover is an expensive piece of kit. I'm sure Terry would like it back in one piece. Don't know if he feels the same way about his wife, though.'

***

They dropped Danny off at a house in Weston Point where Mike had arranged lodgings with Anne, a good soul who didn't ask awkward questions. After introductions were made, Danny settled into his room and decided to take a shower.

Mindful of the bandage on his finger, he stood under the steaming water for a long time, enjoying the heat massaging the back of his neck. He towelled himself dry and changed the dressing on his finger, pleased with how it was healing. A wave of exhaustion overcame him; it had been a long day. Fortunately, it had all gone to plan – simple logistics and a well-prepared team had made it easy. He lay on the bed and drifted off into a deep sleep.

***

Karen got home and found Terry sitting on the only upright chair in the dining room. The bull from the china shop had paid them a visit. She tiptoed through the scattered remains of her best crockery, avoiding the broken glass and furniture as she made her way to his side.

She stood next to him, needing him to get up and hold her, reassure her, do the things any good husband would do, but he didn't. He stared into the distance, breathing heavily. She bent down and kissed him on the cheek.

'I'm okay,' she said. 'They didn't touch me.'

He ignored the kiss and everything it represented and continued to stare at something in the distance.

'What happened?'

She sighed, realising he was not interested in her or her well-being. He just wanted to be angry and vengeful. His lack of empathy left her feeling neglected and unloved. She desperately needed him to comfort her. The reality was that he only cared about himself and his reputation.

She upended the only remaining chair that had four legs and sat down next to him.

'There were two of them,' she began and told him what had happened in as much detail as she could remember.

He didn't move, but his breathing slowed down and became more regular. A good sign.

Forty

Danny woke with a start. The five note jingle from Close Encounters was playing on his phone, alerting him that he had a text message. It was dark, and he rubbed his eyes as he tried to read it.

He'd been dreaming of the painting by Michaelangelo, the Creation of Adam, where God looks down at Adam as they are about to touch. In his dream, the figures morphed into him and Jackie. *It's not getting any easier.* It was 9:02 pm. He'd slept for hours. He looked at the message again but didn't recognise the number.

The text read: It's time to sort things out. Ryan is here answering questions. Come alone. Chilli.

The message contained a location and a time to meet. He got dressed and drove to Sue's house looking for Mike.

'I'll get him for you.' she said. 'Oh, and by the way, that young detective came by, said there's no update on the investigation into Jackie's death, and they're still looking for whoever assaulted me. Honestly, how often do we have to tell them it was that Chilli guy! Anyway, he was here for a couple of minutes and wanted to know where you were. I didn't tell him anything.'

'Was he on his own?' Danny asked. 'Why didn't he just phone?'

'I asked him the same thing,' she said, 'and he said that talking on the phone was uncongenial, whatever that means.'

'It means unfriendly.'

***

Mike, John and Danny drove to the address in Danny's text and parked outside a unit on the Astmoor industrial estate. They got out of the car and walked towards a steel shutter door. It opened before they got to it, and Chilli walked out. He saw Mike and John and sneered.

'My problem is with you Danny, not these pumpkins.'

He looked at Mike and John. 'Do yourselves a favour lads, and piss off.'

They didn't move, and Danny didn't take his eyes off Chilli.

'So, you like hurting women and kids,' Danny said with contempt.

'Ryan's not a kid,' Chilli said. 'If he wants to stand up and be counted, he's got to understand there are consequences. It's just business.'

'I'll be sure to remember that,' Danny retorted. 'So what happens now? You going to deliver me to Terry like a good little boy and have a bit of fun kicking the shit out of me on the way?'

Chilli smiled.

'It's not going to happen,' Danny said. 'I won't be going anywhere with you.'

Chilli shook his head in disbelief. He didn't want to admit it, but he was starting to respect Danny Valik. He had confidence and a way about him that just made him seem like a good guy, someone he could get along with if circumstances were different.

Chilli turned his head slightly towards the unit, and Frank stepped out. Danny laughed and shook his head. 'And you told me to come alone.'

Chilli shrugged. 'Like I said, it's just business.'

Danny turned away and walked towards the car.

Chilli took a gun out of his coat pocket and held it at his side.

'Stay where you are. You're not going anywhere.'

Mike and John looked at each other, and without saying a word, moved a couple of steps back and spread out either side of Danny until they were about ten feet apart. They pulled handguns from their jackets and pointed them at Chilli and Frank. Chilli didn't move.

'We're going to walk away before someone gets hurt,' said Danny.

'I really can't let you do that.'

If Terry found out that he hadn't captured Danny again, it would be one failure too many. Chilli raised his gun and took a step forward.

'You're coming with us.'

Danny's eyes widened as he looked at something past Chilli's shoulder. Chilli wasn't going to fall for that old school trick and kept his gun pointed at Danny's chest.

***

That morning, Ryan had been sitting on a bench next to the river contemplating his life. It was almost a month since he'd grabbed Jackie's handbag. So much had happened since then. Baz and Neil spotted him on the bench but did nothing except make a phone call. Ten minutes later, a black Mercedes screeched to a halt next to Ryan. Chilli got out, punched him in the gut, and shoved him into the car.

At the unit on the industrial estate, Chilli had tied him to a chair and kept him there all day questioning him about Danny, but Ryan had nothing to say. Later, a bigger version of Chilli with a bald head and goatee beard arrived, carrying snacks and water.

'Hey Frank, our guest over here is not being very helpful. You got any ideas how we can loosen his tongue?'

Frank stood in front of Ryan and smacked him in the face a few times, almost snapping his neck.

'Maybe he'll tell me what we need to know after I have my lunch,' he chuckled.

They untied Ryan's hands and gave him a bottle of water while they ate their snacks and quietly chatted at the other end of the unit. Ryan saw Frank handing Chilli a gun. While they were distracted he took the opportunity to work at the ropes holding his legs. *I have no idea what I'm gonna do if I get free, but I'm not hanging around here waitin' to get whacked.*

***

Frank crashed to the ground like a broken mast on a storm-battered sailing ship. He was unconscious before his brain had time to react. Ryan dropped the metre-long piece of scaffolding pole and picked up the gun Frank had been holding. Chilli took a step forward but stopped when Ryan pointed the gun at his chest. Chilli slowly put his gun on the ground and put his hands in the air.

Danny ran to Frank and felt for a pulse. He looked into his glazed eyes and turned to Mike.

'Phone an ambulance.'

He took his coat off and put it under Frank's head after placing him in the recovery position.

Danny walked over to Ryan and carefully took the gun from his hand.

'Go and stand with that guy over there,' he said, pointing at John.

Ryan stared at Frank's lifeless body on the ground. Danny kept the gun pointed at Chilli while Mike came over with his phone pressed to his ear and knelt beside Frank.

Danny turned to Chilli. 'Your bitterness is the reason your friend is lying there.'

He lifted his left hand – 'I should kill you for what you've done to me and my family.'

Chilli was breathing heavily, ready for whatever came next.

'I'm a fair man,' Danny continued, 'which doesn't always work out for me, but hey, what's life without a few risks? I'll stay here until I hear the ambulance, and we'll see what happens. They' – he said, pointing at Mike and John – 'won't interfere until they hear the siren. One way or another, I'll be going with them. Let's settle this!'

He gave the gun to John and just managed to sidestep out of the way as Chilli lunged at him. He squared up to Danny, who came at him with his fists up by his face, elbows tucked into his chest like a boxer. Danny hit out with his left fist and connected with the side of Chilli's head. It was more of a slap than a punch with the bandage on his finger, but it was quick and stunned him a little.

Chilli pulled Danny towards himself with his left hand and blasted a right-hander into his stomach. It connected well but didn't bother Danny. He'd started a rigorous sit up and press-up regime in his teens that he'd adhered to for years. *It had been worth it.*

Chilli let go as Danny hit him in the nose with a straight right making it bleed. As he stepped back, he grabbed Danny's arm, pulling him towards his head. Danny managed to twist forward at the last second and felt a glancing blow from the intended headbutt. It hurt but was better than Chilli's huge forehead crushing his face. They both stood back, breathing hard, looking for the next opening. The wail of a siren echoed through the night.

'Danny, let's go!' Mike shouted. Chilli went to grab hold of Danny, but John stepped forward and pointed his gun at Chilli's head.

Chilli watched them leave then went and sat by Frank. His friend's breathing was ragged, and his face was grey. Chilli had a minute to think about how he would explain Franks' condition to the ambulance crew. He would need a lot more time to think about what he was going to say to Terry.

Forty-One

Ryan sat next to Danny in the back of the car and stared through the side window.

After a couple of minutes, he asked, 'Can you stop? I don't feel good.'

'Pull over somewhere quiet,' Danny said.

As soon as the car stopped, Ryan got out and threw up. 'I didn't want any of this,' he said, wiping his mouth as he got back in the car. 'I hope that guy's going to be alright. He's a bastard. I thought they were going to kill me, but I didn't mean to ….'

Danny had seen death. It was a monkey on the shoulder of every soldier who went to war. Assessing the seriousness of a life-threatening injury became second nature, and Danny's experience told him the odds weren't good for the big guy, but he didn't want to worry Ryan.

'You did what you believed to be right at the time – it's okay, but you need to come to terms with it and move on, or it'll haunt you forever.'

'Where do you want us to drop you?' Danny asked.

Ryan gave them an address on the Windmill Hill estate where his mate Karl lived.

***

Gary Lynch had always been jealous of his brother and the ease with which he strolled through life. He felt like he'd grown up in Terry's shadow, but that feeling was going to change. Danny Valik had come onto the scene at just the right time. Gary was keen to stir the pot and tie up loose ends, including Sophie, while everyone was preoccupied with Danny.

He wasn't an idiot. It was obvious that Sophie liked being the centre of attention, using her position as his wife to get what she wanted. She didn't love him and he didn't care. He'd stopped loving her the first time he found out she'd slept with someone else. He was keeping her around until she was no longer useful. She was winding Terry and Karen up tighter than a violin string. They both hated her, which focused their attention on her and not on what he was doing.

Gary had been making small changes in the business, which Terry was too busy to notice. The intervention at the derelict club had almost been a step too far. Terry wasn't happy about it, but Gary pointed out that Chilli had mutilated Danny's finger against orders, and if he hadn't arrived when he did, there might have been a murder and a lot of unwanted attention. Terry eventually accepted his reasoning and dropped the matter.

Gary offered to help out when Karen was abducted earlier that day, but Terry didn't need his help, so he used the time to carry on working behind the scenes. By 11.30 that night he had a perfect plan and a few strong players on his team. It wouldn't be long before he came out of the shadows.

***

Back at the house in Weston Point, Danny went over what had happened at the industrial estate. The outcome wasn't good, but it would have been worse if Mike and John hadn't been there with him. Ryan knocking Frank unconscious had also weighed the odds in their favour. Danny knew a lot about anger and its destructive power. He wanted to help Ryan stay away from it if he could.

He wondered why Terry hadn't called to give him a rundown of what he would do when he finally caught up with him. The lack of communication gave him an uneasy feeling.

He tried to analyse how he felt but fell asleep and dreamed of Jackie and Barcelona. The February temperatures had been in the low twenties, and they were able to wear t-shirts and shorts on their visit to the Spanish city. He'd organised the trip to celebrate his birthday, but his main objective was to ask her to marry him. He proposed on bended knee in Park Guell, looking down over the city. It had been perfect. The dream was a welcome change from the nightmares he'd been having recently.

***

Ryan and Karl talked for hours.

'You're kidding me!' exclaimed Karl.

He jumped out of his chair and began to pace around the room like an excited kid on Christmas morning waiting to open his first present from Santa.

'You pointed a gun at Chilli Edwards?'

Ryan nodded.

'Wow! You've changed. You never said boo to a goose before, but look at you now.'

He sat back down on the sofa next to Ryan.

'Tell me more.'

Ryan thought back to the moment he had picked up Frank's gun and pointed it at Chilli.

'It was heavier than it looked. I've never held a gun before. I mean, how is it possible to hit a target with somethin' that heavy in your hand. I know people do, but it's hard to believe.'

He stared into space.

'At first, I was maybe kinda scared, and then I thought about what he did to me and got angry and the next thing I was pointing the gun at him.'

He grabbed Karl's arm. 'Mate, you should have seen the look on his face! He didn't know what to do. I've never felt like that before. I don't think I could have shot him, but he put his hands up anyway, so it didn't matter. Maybe he was frightened of me! Mate, Chilli Edwards scared of me, Ryan Thomson!'

He laughed. 'Having that gun in my hand gave me so much confidence. I wish I could have held on to it a bit longer.'

Karl saw the look on Ryan's face as he described how he felt and sadly knew what was coming next. He'd seen that same look on other people's faces the first time they held a gun.

Ryan looked him in the eye. 'I want a gun.'

Forty-Two

Assistant Chief Inspector Tustin sat opposite Harry and Steve with a disappointed look on his face. He took a deep breath.

'I have just been informed that last night an ambulance picked up Frank Wharton, the man who broke into Sue Stevens' house, after an anonymous caller said he'd been in an accident. Correct?'

Harry and Steve nodded.

'I've also been told that he's in a coma with a fractured skull. Chilli Edwards was at the scene and apparently told the medics that Frank tripped and hit his head.'

The chief grimaced. 'I don't believe that for a second. The doctors say the fracture was caused by a blow from a heavy object, and the odds of him dying are pretty high.'

He looked at his wife smiling up at him from the framed photograph on his desk. 'I am even more peeved to hear that Danny Valik was located in North Wales but not arrested. Correct?'

The two detectives in front of him dropped their heads. The Chief leant forward in his chair and slammed his fist onto the desk.

'You have no idea of the shit storm that is raining down on me from above! I need results, gentlemen, and I need them now!'

He sat back in his chair and steepled his fingers.

'As you know, after Jackie Valik died, social media began speculating that a killer was running loose around town. If this carries on, it won't be long before it becomes front-page news, and we'll all look like incompetent idiots!

'Understand this. You two can forget about going home to your families until Danny Valik is arrested – by any means necessary. I've assigned extra officers to the case. There will be severe consequences if this isn't resolved quickly.'

***

Terry had always believed that a generous amount of luck was the reason why Danny Valik was always just out of reach. It would explain his escape from Chilli and Frank, but taking Karen in broad daylight and getting away with it took planning and precision, qualities that most common criminals didn't have. *So who is he working for?*

Terry's informant told him that Danny had been in the Territorial Army for a few years and posted to Afghanistan. *That explains a lot. Most of my men are ex-army, but I can't see any of them successfully planning and carrying out a kidnapping in a car park, avoiding cameras and security. It has got to be luck, and it ends today.*

Terry was losing face, and it wouldn't end well if he didn't stop the rot. Someone, sooner or later, would take advantage, and his empire would come tumbling down around him. It had already started. Members of a rival mob had recently severely beaten one of his men for no apparent reason. They'd approached him in a bar in the city, took him outside and kicked the shit out of him. They didn't care who saw or recorded them. It was one of the other bosses in the city testing the water, poking him to see if they could get a reaction – just business. Terry acted swiftly with a show of strength. When he found out it was a mob from the docks area, he ordered his men to find a member of their crew and hurt him.

'Don't kill him, but make sure his injuries are more severe than our man's.'

Terry sent Chilli and a couple of his men to a gang member's house, and in front of his wife and kids, beat him badly, broke his leg, and rearranged his face. The other mobs got the message – it wasn't personal. Now was not the time to poke Terry Lynch. Everyone kept their distance, watching and waiting for events to unfold.

***

Danny woke to the sound of banging at the front door, followed by a voice shouting 'Police!' and Anne cursing loudly. He jumped out of bed and started to grab some clothes. He heard someone mention a warrant and then footsteps running up the stairs.

'Police!' the same voice shouted through the bedroom door. 'Open up!'

Danny sighed and opened the door. A police officer stood in front of him wearing full riot gear, looking at him through a massive plexi-glass shield.

Danny smiled. 'Good morning, Officer. Have you brought my morning cuppa?'

The man behind the shield moved forward to allow two of his fellow officers into the room. One of the officers pulled Danny's arms down behind his back and cuffed him.

'Any chance I can put my socks and undies on? Can't go out in my jim jams, can I.'

The officer behind the shield nodded.

Danny grinned. 'You'll have to untie me.'

As he finished dressing, the officer read him his rights. They cuffed him again and herded him downstairs towards a Black Maria waiting outside. He nodded to Anne on the way out and mouthed, 'thank you.'

They drove him to the concrete police station next to the unsightly concrete shopping centre, where the desk sergeant took Danny's details and the contents of his pockets. They removed his handcuffs and put him in a cell.

'Detective Inspector Latchford is on his way to interview you.'

Danny sat on the chair and contemplated his predicament. He was doing a lot of that lately. Remembering his life with Jackie was good, but those memories always ended with the sad truth that she was no longer around.

By Danny's reckoning, an officer came for him about an hour later and took him to an interview room with a table, three chairs, two police officers and a recording machine. He sat opposite the two officers.

'DI Latchford,' Danny said with a smile. 'And DC Richards,' he added, nodding at Steve. 'How can I help?'

Forty-Three

The inspector pressed the record button on the machine and read Danny his rights. He explained that the tape machine was there to protect them all from any false accusations.

'The time is now 9:40 am,' the inspector said for the benefit of the tape, and so began the formal interview.

'Danny, tell us what happened the night of Jackie's death. Start with your visit to the Clarendon, where it all seems to have started.'

Steve made notes as Danny told them everything he could remember. They questioned him about different aspects of his story, cross-referencing what he told them against other peoples statements.

Danny sighed a lot and seemed to be distracted. After a while, Steve looked at the inspector and made a drinking gesture with his hand.

Harry nodded. 'The time is now 10:53 am. I am pausing the interview for a toilet break.'

'I'll get the drinks in,' Steve said. He took their orders and left the room. When he returned, they resumed the interview. Although Danny was becoming more and more frustrated, the inspector insisted they account for every detail to ensure that the coroner had no objections to releasing Jackie's body from the morgue.

'And you believe,' the inspector said, 'that the bruising on Jackie's arm was as a result of you grabbing hold of her to stop her falling earlier that night?'

Danny nodded.

The inspector sighed.

'For the benefit of the recording, can you please answer the question, Danny?'

Danny took his time. 'Yes, I believe the bruising happened as I tried to stop my wife from falling on the floor when she nearly fainted.'

Eventually, Steve stood up and started pacing around the room, rubbing the back of his neck.

'He hasn't changed his original statement in any way since we started the interview, Sir. We should stop the tape and let him go.'

The inspector looked at the clock on the wall. 'Very well, I am now terminating the interview and the time is 11:32 am. I'm giving Mr Valik a sheet of paper that contains information on how he can obtain an audio copy of this interview if he needs it.'

The inspector gave Danny the paper then pressed the stop button on the recorder. He took out the two tapes, sealed one and got Danny to sign and date it.

'We'll keep it sealed until it's required and use the other one to transcribe this interview, won't we Steve?' he smiled.

Steve gave him a sarcastic grin, knowing how long it would take to type it using his two-fingered technique.

'Come on, Danny, I'll show you out.'

Danny stood. 'So what happens now, Inspector? Can I arrange Jackie's funeral?'

'We'll give your statement to the coroner with our recommendation.'

'And what will your recommendation be, Inspector?'

'I'll let you know once I've informed the coroner. We're still looking into the other incidents. As I said, we'll contact you in due course.'

Danny's shoulders slumped, and his head dropped. Keeping up a brave face with the odds stacked against him took a lot of energy, which he didn't have at the moment. He took a deep breath, stood straight and followed Steve.

Danny collected his belongings from the front desk and they headed down a corridor towards stairs at the back of the building that led to the parking area.

'Why are we going this way and not the way we came in?' he asked.

'Procedure,' said Steve. 'In through the front, out through the back.'

'How come?' Danny asked.

'A few years ago, a suspected paedophile was brought in and questioned. We eventually let him go whilst we made further enquiries. Unfortunately, someone saw him walk into the station and alerted the family of the girl who accused him of taking pictures of her. They got here and kicked the shit out of him when he came out of the station. By the time we managed to stop them, the guy was in a right mess. We had to call an ambulance. He had broken bones and internal injuries. We do it this way now.'

Danny smiled. 'Vigilante justice. I'd probably do the same if someone hurt my family, wouldn't you?'

Steve looked at him. 'I'd make sure the suspect was found guilty first. Then I'd let the justice system take care of it.'

Danny kept smiling. 'That sounds like police talk to me, something that's drilled into you as soon as you sign on the dotted line.'

Steve turned to him. 'Did you know that vigilante comes from the Latin word vigilare, which means 'to stay awake or to keep watch?' It doesn't mean 'kick the shit out of someone.''

Danny's smile disappeared. 'I do. I went to a Catholic boys school. Learning Latin was compulsory.'

Steve continued. 'The danger with self-appointed vigilantes is that they sometimes go after innocent people, which is what happened to the guy that had the shit kicked out of him. By the time we knew it was a case of mistaken identity, his life had been destroyed. I wouldn't be okay with that on my conscience.'

***

Ken was part of the scenery at the station, like the 20 year old bonsai tree on the Inspectors desk. He loved his job as a security guard and liked to think that he brought a ray of sunshine into the stressful lives of the people who worked at the station. His sense of humour was dry, so he'd been told, but whatever it was, he was always able to put a smile on peoples faces.

He was on the day shift in the gatehouse today – a bit boring, but he didn't complain; he just got on with it. Unemployment and social deprivation levels were high in Runcorn, so he never took his job for granted. He'd be 62 next birthday and was seriously considering retirement. He wanted to spend more time at home with Cath, and they'd worked out they could manage on his pension. Happy days.

He saw the unmarked car approaching from inside the compound and pressed the big green button to open the gate and let it out. He noticed the black Range Rover heading for the gate as the police car went out, so he pressed the red button to stop the gate from closing. It wasn't a police vehicle and whoever was in it needed to sign in. The Range Rover pulled past the gatehouse and stopped on the gate tracks. Ken let go of the button, and the gate stayed where it was while he got up to go and have a word with the driver.

***

Danny and Steve reached the bottom of the stairs that led into the car park. There were cars and vans lined up along three sides of the compound, with the gate and gatehouse occupying the fourth side. Danny saw a couple of coppers get into an unmarked, black BMW and head out the gate as a black Range Rover with blacked-out windows approached and stopped next to the gatehouse. The guy getting out of the car looked familiar, causing Danny to stop mid-stride. Steve stopped next to him.

'What's up?'

'We need to get back into the station. Now!' Danny urged.

Steve saw the look in his eyes and turned to go with him. It didn't feel like the right time to ask questions. They ran back towards the station door.

Ken left his booth to ask the driver to move the car off the tracks and sign in. A man got out of the passenger seat and shook his head at Ken in a 'not a good idea' sort of way, but Ken had a job to do and continued walking towards the car. *Who does this guy think he is, shaking his head at me.*

Realising Ken wasn't going to stop, the guy took a gun from inside his coat and held it at his side while two guys got out the back. Ken stopped. The guy with the gun smiled and shrugged his shoulders. Ken swung around and headed back to the gatehouse.

Steve got to the door ahead of Danny. He pressed the buzzer, looked up at the camera and waited for the desk sergeant to release the lock. Two men from the car reached them and grabbed Danny. He broke free and got a couple of good punches in the face of one guy, but the other guy punched him in the stomach, making him double over.

***

Inside the gatehouse, Ken shut and locked the door behind him, then pressed the other big red button at the side of the desk. An ear-splitting siren began to wail around the car park, echoing off the concrete walls. The gunman frowned and shook his head at Ken again. He shouted at the two men fighting with Danny to hurry up, then raised his gun and fired a couple of shots at the gatehouse in frustration.

When Ken first took the job, they said that the glass in the gatehouse was bulletproof. He hadn't truly believed it until today. *What a great story to tell the grandkids.* The siren made it impossible to hear what the frustrated gunman was shouting, but Ken knew he couldn't repeat it in polite company. He also knew the CCTV cameras would be recording everything but out of habit he wrote down the vehicle's registration number.

Then a little devil appeared on his shoulder and whispered in his ear. He grinned and pushed the manual 'close gate' button on the panel in front of him. He kept his hand on the button as the gate slid along the tracks, ignoring what the sensors were telling it. The gunman jumped into the car just before the gate slid into his door. It hadn't been moving quickly, but it was heavy and made a few dents and scratches.

***

Danny was bent over, being pulled towards the Range Rover by one assailant, and Steve was grappling with the second assailant as the station door finally opened. Three officers rushed out with batons in their hands. One of them went for the guy fighting with Steve, and the other two headed towards Danny.

Once Steve was clear, he saw the other two officers beating the guy dragging Danny. One police baton hit him on the arm, and the other caught him on the thigh. He let out a cry of pain, released Danny and ran to the Range Rover.

The driver of the Range Rover got out and fired a shot into the air. Everyone stopped and looked around.

'Get in the car,' he shouted to his men.

The guy who had initially been fighting with Steve shook off the copper holding him and ran toward the car. There was a loud screeching noise as the Range Rover backed away from the gate with its four assailants. It would need more than a bit of filler and paint to sort out the damage to the bodywork. Ken's little devil was sniggering.

The five good guys stood by the door that led up the stairs into the station. Everyone seemed okay. Danny was just winded, and Steve had taken a couple of punches but nothing serious. The three officers were none the worse for their experience.

The siren stopped wailing as Ken walked over to them.

'Don't worry, lads, I'm okay,' he said sarcastically, then broke into a huge grin.

'What the hell was that? Did someone forget to pay a bill?'

Forty-Four

'Mate, you don't need a gun,' Karl said for the third time. 'It'll be more trouble than it's worth, trust me. Who are you going to kill, anyway? Anyone I know?' Karl was grinning, trying to play it down, but Ryan was like a dog with a bone.

'I know what you're doing,' Ryan said, 'but I've been thinkin' about it a lot, and I want a gun. Don't worry, I'm not gonna kill anyone. It'll be insurance, that's all.'

He raised the cast on his left arm. 'Like I said, This ain't happenin' again.'

'Well, learn kung fu or somethin,' Karl said.

Ryan laughed. 'You said you can get a gun, so get me a gun. Just as long as I don't have to rob a bank to pay for it.'

***

Whilst Ken went to check the gate, Steve and the others went back to the front desk, where a few officers were standing around watching Ken on the car park monitor.

'We're just setting up to watch the CCTV footage,' the inspector said. 'We'll get the registration of the vehicle and the name of the registered keeper. Is everyone okay?'

They all nodded.

The officer hitting the keys on his keyboard swore and called the inspector over.

'There's no footage, Sir. The cameras haven't been recording for the last hour.'

There were a few expletives, and Harry turned to the desk sergeant.

'Get the technical guys to find out what happened, get statements from the three officers who came to Danny's rescue and while it's still fresh in their minds, get descriptions of the bad guys, beards, tattoos, that sort of thing.'

The sergeant raised an eyebrow. Harry put his hands up.

'I know it's a long shot, but we might get something we can use. Steve, you do the same. Get it written down as soon as you can.'

Steve sighed and turned to Danny.

'Do you want a lift home before I start writing up my statement?'

Danny nodded, and they headed back to the car park.

***

The meeting with Gary hadn't gone well. He couldn't put his finger on it, but Terry had the feeling that his brother was stalling for some reason. They couldn't agree on Sophie, and Gary did not appear supportive of his plans for the future. It seemed like he had his own agenda.

Terry heard that bosses from rival gangs around the city were setting up meetings without him. This news and the recent test of his resolve probably meant they were planning a takeover. It wasn't something he could ignore. He needed Gary by his side, but he would do what needed to be done, on his own if necessary. He wouldn't give up his empire without a fight.

***

Gary was pleased after the meeting with Terry. It had gone just as he had planned it. Their differences were becoming more and more apparent. Gary had to do something to ensure his brother stayed focused on something other than the day-to-day stuff, where he had made subtle changes that would only become apparent when he made his move. Sophie had become the wrong kind of distraction for Terry in that respect. He would have to sort her out himself.

He asked her if she'd like to go for a meal at her favourite restaurant, which was how they came to be together in his car driving through narrow country lanes in Cheshire.

'This is nice,' she said, checking her make-up in the sun visor mirror. 'It's been a long time since we had a night out together.'

He smiled, keeping his eyes on the road. At the next crossroads, he turned left.

Sophie put her lipstick away and gave him a sideways glance. 'The restaurant isn't this way. You should have gone straight ahead at the crossroads.'

'I know,' he said.

Sophie looked at him with wide-open eyes. 'Where are we going?'

***

In the car back to Weston Point, Steve explained what would happen next.

'It won't be long before we can let you know about the murder charge and the other incidents involving Chilli Edwards and Jason Lynch. Chilli reported the assault but never gave us a statement, and Jason's statement just doesn't add up. There's no proof to back up his claim that you pushed Jackie off the balcony. Also, now that you've given us your statement, the warrant for your arrest has been rescinded.'

'Rescinded?' Danny asked.

'Cancelled. Overturned.'

They were silent for a little while.

'I didn't want to ask before, but what happened to your finger?'

Danny held up his hand and examined his little finger as if it were a glass of fine wine. It was itchy, and the bandage needed changing, but he could move it about without it hurting too much. He knew it could have been a lot worse.

He didn't see any harm in telling Steve what had happened. 'My new friend Chilli thought I'd be better off without it.'

Steve shot him a glance. 'You didn't report it to the police then?'

Danny shook his head. 'You wouldn't have been able to do anything.'

Steve was about to protest, but Danny held up his hand and smiled.

'When I say you, I mean the police wouldn't have been able to do anything, not you personally.'

Steve nodded as Danny continued.

'There were no witnesses to speak of, and I was in enough trouble. I didn't want to make it worse. One of the men that helped Chilli do this to me was in the Range Rover just now. That's why I said to get back in the station.'

Steve concentrated on driving.

'Was it you who put Frank Wharton in the hospital?'

'No, that wasn't me.'

'Do you know who it was?'

'Yeh, I do, but don't ask me for a name.'

'Who told Chilli to hurt you?' Steve asked. 'Was it Terry Lynch?'

Danny nodded, and Steve shook his head. 'You don't want that guy on your back, believe me.'

Danny stared out of the window. 'Tell me something I don't know.'

He was physically and mentally exhausted. It felt like a knife was being permanently held at his throat, and if he relaxed, it would cut him and kill him. There was no relief from the pressure. He wanted to put Jackie to rest and get on with his life. It's what she would have wanted too, but he couldn't. Not yet.

Steve dropped him at Anne's house and headed back to the station.

Surprisingly, Anne hugged him when he walked in the door.

'Are you okay?' she asked.

Danny smiled. 'Yes, I'm okay. Sorry about what happened this morning. They were a bit over the top, weren't they. Hope they didn't damage anything.'

'Only my pride,' she said. 'I didn't know what to do.'

'You did okay' he said 'and thanks for the warning.'

Forty-Five

Steve got back to the station and found Harry sitting at a table in the canteen with a cup of tea. He went to the drinks machine, got a coffee and joined him.

'So, did we find out what happened to the CCTV?'

The inspector shook his head. 'Everything looks okay with the system. Nothing's broken. The IT lads checked for software glitches and found nothing.'

Steve shook his head.

The inspector stirred his brew. 'To make matters worse, Ken came up to the front desk while you were out. He wrote down the registration number of the Range Rover but forgot all about it while he was inspecting the gate. It was about half an hour before he told us. We put it out on the car radios straight away but no one's reported seeing it.'

'What about the registered keeper?'

'The registration number didn't come up on the DVLA database. Must have been false number plates.'

They sat staring into their drinks when Harry suddenly sat bolt upright.

'Were they wearing masks?'

Steve shook his head.

'Why weren't they wearing masks?' the inspector asked.

Steve shrugged. 'Because they didn't care who saw them?'

Harry stood up. 'They must have known the CCTV wasn't working.'

'How could they know that?'

Harry leant forward and lowered his voice. 'Because somebody told them.'

***

After having something to eat, Danny headed to Sue's house. He phoned ahead to let her know he was on his way. She met him at the door and gave him his second hug of the day. Once she'd let go, they went into the living room where Mike was waiting. Danny told them about the day's events.

'It all sounds like something out of a James Bond film,' Sue said. 'At least you're safe now.'

'Yes, but for how long,' Danny asked. 'Terry Lynch isn't going to stop until he shows everyone that nobody gets away with hurting his family or making a fool of him. I'm a symbol of his failure, a constant reminder that he's not in control, and the longer it goes on, the more desperate he's going to get.'

Mike nodded. 'So, what do you have in mind?'

'Is the tracker you put on the Range Rover still working?'

***

Sophie tried to get out of the car, but Gary had locked it when they got in.

'What made you think you could get away with shaming me,' he asked, eyes fixed on the road. 'Do you think it's okay to sleep with other men when you're married to me?'

He slammed his fist on the steering wheel and screamed. 'Answer me, bitch!'

She didn't reply. She grabbed hold of the steering wheel and pulled it towards her. A crash might help her escape or maybe even kill him. The car screeched from side to side as Gary wrestled with her to regain control.

He punched her in the face, knocking her unconscious.

She woke up face down on the ground with her hands and feet tied together. The tape across her mouth prevented any chance of screaming for help. The light was fading and she was cold. She shivered as she saw a ghostly apparition standing next to a gravestone holding a spade. The figure turned and ambled towards her.

'It didn't have to end this way, Sophie,' said Gary with regret. 'I loved you.'

As she tried to roll away, the spade sliced the top of her head off.

He buried her three feet down on top of his dad's grave. He'd gone to the cemetery earlier that morning with a spade and a rake and made a big show of turning the soil and removing the weeds.

He cleaned the blood off the spade, took the white paper suit, gloves and overshoes off, and put them all into a plastic bag in the boot of his car. He drove to the restaurant, and parked as far away from the entrance as he could. He went in and confirmed his booking.

'You booked a table for two, Sir?' the waiter said, checking the reservation.

'Yes, my wife's just sat in the car checking her makeup. She'll be here in a minute. Can I have a couple of gin and tonics while we wait for our table?'

After about ten minutes, the waiter let him know that his table was ready.

With no sign of his wife he said 'I'll go and find out why she's taking so long.'

He went out to the car, walked around and shouted her name a couple of times near the CCTV cameras. He told the waiter he'd looked everywhere but couldn't find her. One of the waitresses went to check the ladies toilets, but she wasn't there.

He phoned the police and reported her missing. They informed him that they would have to wait 24 hours before filing a missing persons report. *Job done!*

Forty-Six

Ryan handed the money to Karl and became one of the 875 million civilians in the world who owned a handgun. It was a Browning L9A1, a high powered, single-action semi-automatic handgun. It was the standard British military issue sidearm until 2013, when the Glock 17 replaced it. The changeover meant that thousands of ex-army Browning handguns found their way onto the black market.

Ryan's was black with a wooden grip. He held it in his hand and felt his pulse quicken. He'd paid a few hundred pounds for it, apparently at mates rates, and was confident it was money well spent. Karl showed him how to strip it down, clean it and put it back together.

'How come you know so much about guns?' Ryan asked. 'Have you shot anyone?'

Karl laughed. 'In answer to your first question, I could say a misspent youth, but sometimes it isn't misspent. It all depends on your point of view.'

'And the second question?'

'Maybe,' Karl winked, 'No, I haven't killed anyone, not yet anyway.'

Ryan cradled the gun in his hand. 'Can I try this out for real somewhere? Shoot some bullets '

'Sure, I know somewhere we can go to fire off a few rounds. You ready?'

Karl took the gun from Ryan, wrapped it in a hand towel and put it in his rucksack along with the ammunition.

***

Terry didn't tolerate failure, but he understood that sometimes circumstances made it impossible to do anything other than fail, and on those occasions, it was just bad luck. But failing to capture Danny Valik after three attempts was unacceptable.

His contact had given him a heads up. Danny had been arrested and was at Runcorn police station. He sent four men to pick him up and bring him back. If they'd done their job, Danny would have been in the Range Rover with them when they got back, but he wasn't.

He saw the state of the Range Rover when his men returned.

'Get that under cover and get it repaired ASAP. You are so lucky it's not my new baby.'

Terry wasn't feeling confident about the men around him at the moment. There was too much at stake, and they didn't have the luxury of second or third chances.

***

Karen had tried to set up a meeting between her husband and her son. She wanted Jason to come home and see his dad, but he'd refused to go back, despite his mother's pleas. Everyone had underestimated Danny Valik.

Her abduction had been all too real, and Jason didn't want the same thing happening to him.

Terry didn't leave his house unless there was good reason, but Karen pleaded with him, so he contacted Chilli and arranged a meeting in Runcorn with him and Jason the next day.

***

Kidnapping Karen had not changed anything. Danny expected a call from Terry, but that hadn't happened. It became clear that Terry wasn't going to stop until he had his revenge, no matter who got hurt along the way. Danny had to go on the offensive to make sure Terry left him and his family alone.

Forty-Seven

Jason met Chilli at the industrial unit an hour before Terry arrived.

'Be nice to your dad when he gets here' said Chilli. 'There's no point having a slanging match with him. He's coming to sort things out with you, so let him sort it. And if he mentions Danny Valik, don't get pissed off and say you're going to find him and hurt him. See what he has to say first. You never know; he might leave it up to us. Okay?'

Jason said nothing.

A car arrived outside. Four doors slammed shut.

Jason looked at Chilli.

'Three or four men? Does he usually bring that many to a meeting?'

'No,' said Chilli.

A man he recognised popped his head through the door and scanned the room, then walked in with his right hand behind his back. He nodded at Chilli, not waiting for an acknowledgement, and spoke over his shoulder to someone outside. Another man walked in. Terry came in next, followed by a third man.

Terry walked over to Chilli and patted him on the shoulder.

'How's Frank?'

'Still in a coma. It's touch and go.'

Terry nodded. 'That's a shame. He's a good soldier.'

He turned to Jason. 'How are you, son?'

**

Mike constantly monitored the tracker he'd placed on the blue Range Rover. Technology these days was like something out of a sci-fi film, verging on the unbelievable. It was sometimes hard to keep up, but he loved it, which made learning about it easy.

The red dot on his phone showed the car on the motorway heading out of Liverpool. He watched as the dot turned onto the dual carriageway heading for the bridge into Runcorn.

He phoned Danny. 'Terry's on the move. I'll let you know if he crosses the bridge.'

He phoned John and then made a third call while walking to his car.

He called the same three numbers when the dot crossed the bridge.

'It's time.'

**

Jason hated his dad calling him son. They weren't close, so it always sounded false and condescending. Jason wanted to laugh but remembered what Chilli had told him.

'I'm okay.'

Terry looked at his son's leg. 'It's getting better?'

Jason sighed. 'What do you want, dad? You haven't come here to find out if my leg is okay.'

Straight to the point. That was different.

Terry cleared his throat. 'Your mum wants us to talk. And she wants you to come home so she can look after you.'

'I'm not going. It's not my home anymore. I'm doing alright here. Just ask Chilli.'

Terry shrugged. 'If you don't want to talk, that's fine with me. I'll let your mum know that we tried. Okay?'

He looked from Chilli to Jason. 'Now, down to business. I need your help.'

Their reactions were a picture. They both looked surprised, then relieved.

'Some bosses want to take me down, and I need people I can trust at my back. Gary's on board, and a couple of the other bosses have agreed to help. Can I count on you two?'

***

Steve's phone rang at about 9 pm. The station phone number number lit up the screen.

'Hi, Connie.' He'd spoken to her before he left for home and knew she was on the switchboard tonight.

'Hi, Steve. I got a call about five minutes ago from one of our unmarked cars following a blue Range Rover along the M62. The registration of the vehicle popped up on the ANPR system. It belongs to Terry Lynch. The officer has been behind it for a while. Thought you might be interested to know where it's going.'

'So tell me.'

'It's headed towards Runcorn. It'll be on the bridge in a few seconds. What do you want him to do?'

'Have you let the inspector know?'

'I can't get hold of him,' she said. 'His phone goes to voicemail.'

'Can you get another unmarked car to follow the Range Rover on the other side of the bridge?'

'Yes.'

'Okay, do that and get the car to call me once it's behind the Range Rover.'

'Will do.'

'And keep trying to get the inspector.'

***

Chilli's phone rang. It was one of his informants. He didn't answer it.

Terry asked again. 'As I said, can I count on your help?'

Chilli and Jason looked at each other, then back at Terry, and nodded.

Terry frowned and began clenching and unclenching his fists. 'What's going on here? Do you need permission from each other to answer a simple question?'

'No, we don't Terry, but we've spent a bit of time working together recently and—'

'Working together? What do you mean, "working together"?' Terry asked. 'Is there something I should know?'

Jason was staring wide-eyed at Chilli. *What are you doing*! *Shut up you idiot!*

Terry began to unconsciously grind his teeth and looked from Chilli to Jason.

Chilli was confused. *Why is Terry pissed off? What's up with Jason?*

'No, Terry, it's nothing to worry about,' he said. 'Jason asked me to help him out. He said you were okay with it.' Terry didn't move or say a word. Chilli put two and two together and turned to Jason. 'You said your dad— ' but the expression on Jason's face told him all he needed to know. The damage was done – his hopes of working with Terry back in Liverpool had been blown out of the water. Trust was everything. Without it, there was nothing.

'Terry,' he said sheepishly, opening his hands in front of him like a priest speaking to his congregation, 'Jason told me he'd spoken to you about it. We were planning how we could help you find Danny Valik.'

Terry looked ready to explode. 'Plans!' he shouted, his face turning red. 'You work for me, Chilli. There's no moonlighting on the side, no one else you make plans with. You work for me!'

Forty-Eight

Ryan couldn't understand what was going on. He'd walked from Karls place to the industrial estate knowing that Chilli was likely to be there. He had tucked the Browning into the back of his jeans, just to make sure there was no chance of him suffering anymore broken bones. It was life insurance. That was all.

He didn't know what he was going to say, but he had to do something to stop Chilli from coming after him for putting his mate in hospital. He spotted Chilli's black Mercedes parked in front of the unit and hid behind some bushes. *Should I go in with my hands up, or should I have the gun out in front of me?*

Another car came around the corner. It was Baz dropping Jason off. *Even better.* It took a little while to work out what he was going to say to them, but just as he got his script together and plucked up the courage to go inside, a blue Range Rover turned up. He stayed hidden and watched four men get out and enter the unit. One of them was Terry Lynch.

***

The officer in the unmarked BMW on the Runcorn side of the bridge phoned Steve.

'I'm behind the Range Rover. It's driving towards Windmill Hill. What do you want me to do?'

'Did Connie manage to speak to the inspector?'

'Don't think so. Hang on. The vehicle has just turned off towards the industrial estate. If I follow, he's bound to spot me. What do you want me to do?'

Steve checked his watch. 'Can you go and park up somewhere until I sort things out? There are shops on Windmill Hill, aren't there? '

'Yes, there are. What do you need to sort? You're in charge. It's your shout.'

'Just park up, and I'll get back to you in a bit. Okay?'

'No problem. Like I said, it's your shout.'

***

Mike caught up with the Range Rover as it came off the bridge. He followed behind a black BMW that that had just slotted inbetween them.

He called Danny. 'Terry's just turned off towards the industrial estate. I'll call you back when I'm parked up.'

The black BMW in front of him continued straight along the carriageway, leaving Mike behind the Range Rover. It turned left at the end of the slip road, went down the carriageway, and turned left onto Arkwright Road. It crossed the traffic lights at the bus lane and headed towards a T junction. Mike pulled into a parking bay in front of a single storey office unit before the T-junction. Both directions were dead ends. He waited for the others to arrive.

***

Jason watched as Terry's face changed from red to purple.

'Dad, this isn't what you think. Me and Chilli wanted to sort out Danny Valik so you don't't have to.'

Terry shook his head. 'Is that why Frank is in a coma? Have you sorted out Danny Valik? No, you have not. He's still free as a bird while we are running around with our pants round our ankles!'

Terry took a slow walk around Jason. 'You make me laugh. It's a game to you, isn't it? Cops and robbers, good guys and bad guys. How does it make you feel, son?'

***

Danny pulled in alongside Mike, turned the engine off and wound his passenger window down.

'Are they still there?'

'Yeh. At the end of the road, turn left, and he's down there somewhere – should be easy to find – there aren't that many Range Rovers around here.'

'Let's wait for John before we make a move.'

Mike nodded. 'He won't be long. And I've spoken to someone else who was keen to give us a hand. He should be here soon.'

Danny frowned. 'Someone else?'

***

Terry was facing the door when a man walked in with his hands in the air.

One of his men pointed his gun at the intruder's chest.

'Who the hell are you?' Terry asked.

Chilli snarled 'It's Danny Valik.'

'What!' Terry shouted.

He turned to face Chilli and Jason. 'How the hell did he know where to find me? Did you tell him we would be coming here? Is this part of your plan, you tossers?'

Danny slowly dropped his hands, ensuring everyone could see what he was doing.

'No one told me you were coming here, Terry. Is it okay to call you Terry?' He smiled and continued without waiting for an answer. 'There are ways of finding people. It wasn't difficult.'

'You've either got balls of steel, Danny boy, or you're stupid because you've made a serious mistake. You should have known your luck was going to run out sooner or later.'

He spoke to the guy closest to Danny. 'Make sure he's clean.'

Danny turned towards the door and whistled loudly.

Mike came in with his handgun pointed at the guy nearest Danny. John followed with a semi-automatic AK47 pointed at Terry.

'Let's keep this friendly,' Danny said. 'We all want to go home, don't we. This began as a neighbour dispute, and here we are pointing guns at each other, my wife is dead, one of your men is in a coma, and part of me is missing. What this tells me, Terry, is that you have an unreasonable desire to exact revenge.'

Terry had to say something. It looked like Danny was running the show. 'You broke my son's leg because he was playing his music too loud. What gives you the right to do that and then abduct my wife? Who do you think you are?'

Danny shook his head. 'We've both made a lot of mistakes, Terry. But just like you, I draw the line at family.'

He pointed at Chilli. 'He slapped my sister around trying to get information about me. If you don't know that, you should ask him. But if you do, then this all comes back to you..'

Danny took a step closer, and all the guns twitched.

'I want your word that this ends here. No more violence. If you decide to pursue this, I'll make sure you regret it.'

No one spoke. A slow handclap from Terry broke the silence.

'Great speech, Danny boy, although I have heard better. I haven't been threatened like that for a long time. People who threaten me don't get the chance to regret what they've said, and neither will you. You've been a pain in the arse for far too long. It's time to get rid of you.' He nodded towards his men.

Forty-Nine

After the Range Rover turned up, Ryan realised it probably wasn't the right time for a chat with Chilli and Jason. He was about to leave when Danny arrived. From his position amongst the trees and bushes, he watched as Danny, Mike, and John walked towards the unit. *What are they doing here?* He was about to step out and greet them, but something stopped him.

The old Ryan wouldn't have thought twice about what was happening, but he cautiously stayed hidden. He peeked around the corner of the unit and saw Mike and John waiting at the door holding uns. *This is serious shit! Danny must be inside*. He heard a loud whistle, and Mike and John went in, guns held in front of them. Then there was silence.

He leant back against the unit and took a deep breath. Under the circumstances, the decision he was about to make wasn't that difficult. He took the safety off his gun and moved towards the door. As he passed the front of the Range Rover, a movement caught his eye. Unlike the back and sides of the vehicle, there was no privacy glass on the windscreen. *Someone is in there*. He held his gun up two-handed and pointed it at the windscreen. He didn't know if bullets would go through the glass, but he waved his gun, indicating that whoever was in there needed to get out. The passenger side rear door slowly opened.

***

As Terry's men were preparing to open fire, there was a scream from the doorway.

'Terry. No!'

It was Karen. She'd waited patiently in the back of the Range Rover and ducked down when she saw Danny Valik and his friends walk into the unit. She didn't know what to do. She went through a few scenarios in her head and decided to stay where she was. As she fidgeted in her seat, a tall guy walked in front of the Range Rover. *What the hell is going on? Who is he?* She hoped that the glass was bulletproof but wasn't prepared to take the chance. She got out when he started waving his gun around.

'Who are you?' Ryan asked. She saw a flicker of recognition on his face when she told him she was Jason Lynch's mum. He didn't know why, but for some reason, he dropped his gun to his side.

'Do you know what's going on in there?' she asked.

'Not really. I was expecting Chilli to be alone.'

'What are you planning to do?' she asked, mindful of the gun in his hand.

Ryan looked at the door to the unit. He didn't want to go in there, but he knew he had to. The gun gave him courage. 'I'll take a look,' he said. 'Go and sit in the car. You'll be safe there.'

'I'm coming with you.' He was too nervous to argue.

***

Terry watched Karen walk in followed by a tall, young guy pointing a gun at her back. Fear swept through him when he saw the cast on the guy's arm and realised it was Ryan Thomson. His adrenalin levels were already high, but with Karen there, they went through the roof. His men had their guns aimed at Danny and his mates and were about to shoot, but now Karen was in the firing line behind Danny.

He shouted as loud as he could, 'Stop!'

The word echoed around the prefabricated building. His heightened senses heard and saw everything in slow motion. No one moved. His men turned their heads towards him, but the tell-tale explosion of a hammer hitting the flat end of a bullet meant that someone had been too quick off the mark.

Terry saw one of his men immediately raise both hands to let everyone know that he'd heard the shout, but there was nothing he could do to stop the bullet. It was intended for Danny, but the shooter had lowered his arm when he heard the shout. No one fell to the ground, and there were no more gunshots. Danny turned around to make sure Mike and John were still standing. He put his hands up again in a calming gesture.

'Just _ relax,' Danny said.

Ryan and Karen both turned white and were rooted to the spot, but as Danny caught her eye, she gave him a dirty look, refusing to let him see she was frightened.

He walked over to her and casually pointed his gun at her head.

Danny gave Terry a determined look. 'Tell your men to drop their guns.'

Terry gave the signal. They placed their weapons on the floor. Mike collected them and put them into a holdall he found under some boxes in the corner of the room. John stayed vigilant and Danny lowered his gun as Ryan came forward and stood next to him. Danny gave him a questioning look when he saw the gun in his hand.

Ryan held his gaze and said, 'Don't hurt her, Danny. She's here to see Jason. She's his mum.'

Danny nodded. Ryan wore his new found confidence with ease, like a tailor fitted suit. It hadn't been there when they'd first met at the garage by the flats, but he'd changed. They needed to talk, but not now.

He turned to face Terry. 'I was right about you, wasn't I Terry. You would have killed my friends and me just now if Karen hadn't walked in. Our lives mean nothing to you.'

Danny shook his head.

'I've seen men die protecting families, friends and their way of life. Good men that would put themselves in harms way if it meant no harm would come to their loved ones. Are you a good man Terry? I don't think so. Take some time to think about what just happened. I won't give you any more chances. I came here to talk to you, but once again, you refuse to listen.'

He looked at Terry for a few seconds and calmly said, 'If there's a next time, I'll kill you.' He turned to Mike and John. 'Let's go'

He grabbed hold of Karen's arm and walked towards the door. She shook her arms to make him let go, but he had a firm grip.

It was Ryan's turn to give Danny a questioning look.

'She's just insurance until we get out of here,' Danny said.

Mike and John covered their exit.

Terry shouted, 'Hurt her, and I'll show you how good a man I can be.'

They had parked their cars some distance away, and Karen was making it difficult for Danny to get away.

Terry's men piled out of the unit and ran to the Range Rover.

'Shit!' Mike shouted. 'They've got more guns. Get a move on!' Danny continued to struggle with Karen. At this rate, they wouldn't make it.

***

The Range Rover roared, tyres screeched, and Terry drove at Danny, his men shooting from the widows. Mike and John returned fire from a kneeling position. Ryan stopped and turned around to help out.

Danny shouted. 'No, Ryan! Stay with me. Those two know what they're doing.'

Gunshots echoed off the sides of the metal units along the road.

Danny shook his head in bewilderment. After everything that Terry had just said, his men were firing indiscriminately at them. Karen was in the firing line again.

There was a boom, louder than any thunder crack, and everyone instinctively ducked their heads. The Range Rover wobbled. There was a dint in the windscreen, but it kept on coming.

'Is that the friend you mentioned earlier?' Danny asked.

'Yeh' Mike shouted. 'It's Colin.'

Fifty

Colin had kept in touch with Mike from Spain, but when Danny's situation got worse, he headed back to England. The plane landed on the tarmac at Manchester airport and, as usual, it was raining. He collected a brand new hire car and drove through the lousy weather to his mum's house – not far from Sue and Mike. He phoned to let her know he was on his way and would be staying with her for a few days.

The first chance he got, he took the lock off the attic door and went up to check his army kitbag. Unlike Danny and Mike, he'd been in the regular army.

He took his time stripping the M16 rifle and reassembling it, making sure it was ready to use.

Mike was surprised but pleased to hear that Colin was back.

'You've arrived at the right time,' Mike said and outlined Danny's plan.

'Sounds risky to me,' Colin said, 'but just let me know when and where you want me, and I'll be there.'

When he got the call from Mike, he took his kit and drove to the bridge. He was a bit late to the party at the industrial estate, but it gave him time to set himself up on top of a shipping container in a lay-by two hundred yards away. He looked through his field glasses from his vantage point and saw Mike and John standing outside the unit and presumed Danny was inside. Mike and John went in, and a tall guy emerged from his hiding place at the side of the building. He stood in front of a blue Range Rover and waved a gun at the windscreen. A dark haired woman eventually got out. They went into the unit together, and a single gunshot sounded from inside.

Colin watched as Danny and the woman came out, followed by the tall guy, then Mike and John. They ran along the road toward their cars, as four men burst out of the unit and piled into the Range Rover. *The bad guys.*

He sighted the scope on his rifle and released the safety. The men began to shoot at his friends from the windows of the Range Rover. He fired at the windscreen and the vehicle swayed from side to side like a ship in a storm.

The hands holding the guns retreated into the Range Rover. Colin took another shot at the passenger front tyre but hit the alloy wheel. He adjusted the sight on the rifle to compensate and took another shot but missed again. The vehicle carried on towards Danny. Colin put the rifle into semi-automatic mode and sprayed the side of the Range Rover with bullets as it passed him.

Danny was happy to hear Colin doing his thing. It would make getting away a lot easier. A sudden stab of pain in his chest took his breath away and almost dropped him to his knees. He took a firm grip on Karens arm and carried on running. Now wasn't the time to stop.

***

Chilli and Jason were left alone in the unit.

'You said you'd spoken to your dad about us working together but you didn't, did you.' said Chilli. 'You just dropped me in a shit load of trouble, you dick.'

After what had just happened, Jason didn't want to be there, and he certainly didn't want to listen to this meathead have a go at him. He pulled his phone out of his pocket and called Baz to come and pick him up. Chilli was pacing around, eyes fixed on Jason. They both looked up as they heard shots fired. Jason began to hobble towards the door.

'Where are you going?'

Jason ignored him, but was pulled back as Chilli grabbed his arm.

'You want to get yourself killed?' he said. 'Stay here for a minute until it goes quiet.'

Jason pushed Chilli's arm away and pointed outside. 'My mum's out there. I'm going to see what's happening.' He continued limping towards the door.

Chilli caught up and grabbed his arm again. 'Stay here, you prick!'

Jason had had enough. He looked Chilli in the eye and said calmly, 'Get out of my way.' Chilli didn't move.

'You know what, Chilli,' said Jason. 'You're pathetic! You think you're someone, but you're nothing! No one gives a toss about you! I don't agree with much of what my dad says, but he's right about you. You're a sad old man; a has been. You think you're the boss in this shitty little town. Don't make me laugh. You're nobody,' he said with a grin. 'Now, get out of my way!'

Chilli hit him in the face, and he fell backwards onto the floor. Jason shook his head and began to laugh. Chilli grunted and knelt on Jason's broken leg. Jason screamed.

'Not laughing now, are you!' Chilli was in the mood to give the kid a good hiding.

Jason punched him in the leg and continued laughing. Chilli looked down and saw blood on the knife in Jason's hand. *Little shit!* He raised his fist to punch Jason again, just as Jason reached up and buried the knife into his right forearm.

Chilli stood up and stared at the knife embedded in his arm. He pulled it out and threw it away before crashing down with both knees onto Jason's chest. He heard a rib crack, and Jason gasped for breath.

A horrible feeling of dizziness caught him off guard as he tried to stand up. He looked down at his leg. There was a lot of blood. *I need to stop the bleeding.* He crawled off Jason and sat on the floor next to him. He put his hand directly on the wound to try and stem the bleeding.

Fifty-One

Danny and the others made it back to their cars in one piece, the staccato burst of Colin's semi-automatic M16 falling silent as their escape was assured. Danny let go of Karen's arm, expecting her to run back to Terry, but she just stood and looked at him.

'You going to shoot me now?' she asked defiantly.

He shook his head. 'No, you're safe. I'm not going to hurt you.' He got in the car with Ryan and reversed onto the main road.

***

Karen heard the Range Rover approaching and turned around to see it thundering along the road in pursuit of Danny. Terry almost didn't see her. The vehicle came to a juddering halt next to her as he slammed on the brakes.

'Get in!' he shouted through the open window.

She hesitated. She could tell by the look on his face that he was hellbent on killing Danny, and nothing was going to get in his way. She'd seen that same look several times during their marriage and hadn't understood it at first, but she wasn't stupid. She soon realised that he had that look in his eyes when he was about to kill someone. 'Never ask someone to do something you wouldn't do yourself,' he used to say.

She never told him what she suspected. She didn't want to see him look at her that way one day. She stepped away from the vehicle. Terry looked puzzled.

'I'll go back and get Jason,' she said. 'I'll call for someone to pick us up.'

Terry shook his head and drove away without a second glance.

***

Danny phoned Mike. 'It'll be better if we split up. I'm pretty sure he'll come after me, but I'll give him the slip and meet you and John at Wigg Island car park later.'

At the junction, Mike turned left.and Danny turned right. His car was no match for the Range Rover that now followed him. He would have to use his local knowledge of the area to even things up. Danny watched as the lights of the Range Rover got brighter in the rear-view mirror until they were so close they disappeared. The car lurched forward. It didn't have much in the way of reinforced protection and couldn't take more knocks like that without sustaining severe damage. As Terry tried to come alongside them, Danny moved across the narrow road to block him.

Ryan had done nothing up until this point. So Danny was surprised when he opened his window and lifted himself onto the door until he faced backwards. He then fired three shots at the front of the on-coming Range Rover.

'Get back inside!' Danny shouted. They were approaching a roundabout with metal direction signs that would have taken Ryan's head off. Danny swerved past the roundabout and managed to get back onto the straight bit of the road. The tightness across his chest began to worry him.

Terry drove straight over the roundabout.

Ryan went to take another shot.

'Aim for the tyres if you can,' Danny shouted over the screeching engine. Ryan fired another three shots. None of them hit a tyre. He had seven bullets left and no spare magazines. It was something to remember for next time – if there was a next time.

***

Terry rammed them again, and Ryan flopped back inside. Danny went left onto a country road that led to the dual carriageway where they turned left again. The straight bit of road leading to the next roundabout was a problem as the Range Rover was a lot faster than Danny's car. They approached the roundabout side by side, but Danny managed to get round first and headed through one of the new housing developments that led onto a country road.

He was heading for the arched, single lane brick-walled bridge over the canal on Delph Lane. It was a narrow bridge. He'd squeezed over it in a car before and hoped the Range Rover would be too wide to get across. They went under the railway bridge and Danny could see the canal bridge up ahead. He prayed that nothing was heading their way from the other side.

They hit it at speed and flew through the air with all four wheels off the ground. Ryan braced himself against the dash but still hit his head on the roof when they landed.

The Range Rover had been going too fast to stop when Terry realised it wasn't going to get across. It was now held tightly between the stone arms of the bridge and Terry was shifting gears from 4 wheel to 2 wheel drive to try and escape.

***

Karen went into the unit and saw Chilli lying on the floor in a pool of blood. Jason was standing over him.

'Are you okay?' she asked.

He nodded.

She looked down at Chilli's lifeless form. 'Is he dead?'

Jason nodded again.

'He came at me with a knife. We struggled, and he fell on it. It was an accident. I made a tourniquet to stop the bleeding' – he pointed at the rag on Chilli's leg – 'but it didn't do any good. He just died.'

She saw the finger and thumb on his left hand tapping to a rhythm that only he could hear. Terry wasn't the only one who could read their son.

'Have you called an ambulance?'

He shook his head.

She took out her phone and dialled the Emergency Services.

Jason snatched it from her. 'We don't need an ambulance. I'll sort it.'

'If you don't call an ambulance, it's murder.'

'And if I do, I'll go to jail for manslaughter. I'm not doing time 'cos of him.'

Karen was helpless as she watched her son stand at a crossroads and make the wrong choice.

'Jason, you'll be a murderer. Don't do this. Phone an ambulance, please,' she begged, pushing the phone into his hand.

A car pulled up outside. 'That's Baz,' he said ignoring her.

He looked down at Chilli. 'I'll sort this.'

A cold shiver trickled down her spine as she saw the look in his eyes. He didn't realise it yet, but he was his father's son, and the choices he was making would lead him to a dark and uncertain future.

Fifty-Two

Terry had watched Danny's car fly over the bridge, just missing the sides, and realised too late that the Range Rover was too wide to get across. He would have stopped and checked the clearance any other time, but his single-minded obsession didn't allow for that. They were stuck like a cork in a bottle. Terry's men hadn't moved.

'Get out!' he shouted at the two men on the back seat. 'What do I pay you lot for? Kill the bastards!'

'Boss, we can't open the doors.'

Terry punched the steering wheel in frustration. 'Pull the seat down and get out at the back. I'll open it from here.'

They pulled the back seat forward and managed to remove the parcel shelf.

Terry said to the man sitting next to him. 'Get your head out of the window and start shooting.'

***

Ryan saw the hatch at the rear of the Range Rover open. 'Shit! They're coming out of the back. Let's go!'

They'd stayed too long, but Danny didn't feel too good. His heart was a hammer in his chest, doing its best to break out.

'Can you drive?' he asked. Ryan shook his head. He hadn't had time to notice before, but Danny didn't look well. His face was pale, and his breathing shallow.

'What's wrong?'

Danny didn't get a chance to reply as the stillness of the night succumbed to the sound of gunfire. Ryan grabbed Danny's arm and helped him to the front of the car. His breathing had become ragged and laboured.

'I'll be alright in a minute,' he said. 'Just need to get my breath back.'

Ryan took a peek and saw two men firing at them from behind the Range Rover.

'Don't worry about them,' Danny said. 'They can't get past the car. They'd have to cross the canal to get to us.'

Ryan could see another way, but he didn't want to worry Danny. The passenger in Terry's car also began spraying bullets at them.

***

Colin had been able to follow the Range Rover along the narrow country roads, but his rented Vauxhall Corsa struggled to keep up on the faster stretches of road. He lost sight of them going through the new housing estate, but took the Daresbury turn-off down a road he knew well. There was a narrow bridge across the canal about half a mile away, which would make it near impossible for a vehicle the size of a Range Rover to cross. Danny would know that. He put his foot down.

***

Ryan aimed his gun at the men behind the Range Rover.

'Do you know how to use that?' asked Danny, pointing at the gun in Ryan's trembling hand.

'I've had a go,' he said. 'My mate showed me. We went to the Yorkshire Moors and fired at some trees in the middle of nowhere.'

Danny looked doubtful. 'Shooting at trees and cars is different to shooting at people. Trees and cars don't shoot back, and they don't die from bullet wounds. You hit one of these guys, and chances are you'll kill him.'

He let that sink in for a few seconds and grimaced as the band around his chest grew tighter.

'Why don't you put a couple of rounds over their heads so we can get in the car. You don't want to kill anyone today Ryan.'

'I've only got seven bullets left.'

He handed Ryan his gun. 'Just use one at a time, and then use mine. I'm feeling a bit better,' he lied. 'Let's get out of here. Take a shot now.'

Ryan fired a shot over the heads of the two men behind the vehicle. They instinctively dropped down, giving Ryan time to grab hold of Danny and pull him round to the driver's door. Ryan fired another couple of shots as he moved round to the passenger side.

The return fire began again. The rear window shattered. They stayed as low as they could while the car limped away. Ryan watched the two gunmen climb onto the roof of the Range Rover. *Thought so!*

***

Colin saw the Range Rover ahead, stuck in the middle of the hump-backed bridge. The revving engine and screeching tyres covered the sound of his approach. He stopped the car about 100 yards away and saw two men firing shots over the bridge.

He settled behind a giant oak tree at the side of the road, got the M16 from his kit bag, unfolded the metal stock and inserted a full magazine into the receiving chamber. He fired a short burst over the heads of the two men just to get their attention. They ducked, turned around and returned fire. Colin stayed put until the shooting stopped. When he looked again, the men had moved to the front of the Range Rover. It was edging forward, almost free of the bridge.

Colin moved toward a tree 50 yards ahead. A shot hit the tree next to him and he saw the front seat passenger firing through the window at him. He returned fire and made it safely to cover, then put the rifle into single-shot mode, and sighted the gunman's arm. He fired and heard a scream as the arm disappeared back into the vehicle. He scurried to the next oak tree.

***

The two men at the front of the Range Rover shot at Danny and Ryan as they attempted to drive away. Ryan fired his last two bullets out of the back of the car, this time aiming for the men, but he missed. There was a loud bang, and the car dropped to one side as one of the tyres burst. It swerved to the left and stalled as it hit a tree. Danny was trying to get it going again, but the noises coming from the engine suggested that it wasn't going anywhere, anytime soon.

Danny spluttered. 'It's knackered, and me along with it.'

His eyes were screwed tightly shut as he clutched his chest.

'Make a run for it, Ryan. It's me_ they want.'

Ryan was at a crossroads. He had a choice and he made it. He grabbed Danny's gun and began to fire at the approaching men. They were caught by surprise and he managed to hit one of them in the leg. The man hit the ground writhing in pain. The other continued to shoot at them but stopped and looked over his shoulder when he heard a change in the noise coming from the engine of the Range Rover. Inch by battered inch, Terry had finally freed it from the bridge.

Ryan took the opportunity to shoot at the man while he was distracted. The bullet hit him just under his right armpit, and he dropped like a stone. Ryan stood up. *Is he dead? Did I kill him?* He began to walk, trancelike, toward the man on the ground.

"No!" Danny tried to shout. Ryan turned and saw Danny leaning on the car. He was waving at Terry, who had stepped out of the Range Rover and was pointing a gun at Ryan. 'Get_back_ here!' Danny gasped.

Ryan heard a gunshot and felt his right shoulder jump. The gun fell out of his hand. Terry walked forward, gun held high, pointing at Ryan's head. Ryan squeezed his eyes shut and heard the gunshot. When he opened his eyes, Terry was face down on the ground.

Ryan looked towards the bridge and saw someone with a rifle walking towards him. He passed the man Ryan had shot in the leg, took his gun from him and told him not to move. He then knelt beside the other guy Ryan had shot and felt for a pulse. His head dropped.

He went to Ryan and said 'I'm Colin. I'm here for Danny.' He walked to where Danny was leaning on the car and helped him to sit down. Danny was sweating and breathless, but he was able to smile as Colin knelt beside him.

'Hello, mate,' he whispered.

Colin smiled. 'Hang in there, Danny. We'll get you an ambulance.'

Ryan came over. 'Is he dead? The man that I shot. Is he dead? '

Colin looked up and nodded. Ryan's shoulders slumped, and his head hung shamefully.

Colin commanded. 'Sit down before you fall down and put some pressure on that wound.'

He turned to Danny. 'You both need an ambulance.' He made the call.

Fifty-Three

'They're on their way,' Colin said, taking his coat off and placing it under Danny's head. 'I can't do much for you at the moment, mate. You've not been shot. Is it your heart?'

Danny nodded.

'We've got a lot of catching up to do, me and you. Maybe after all this gets sorted, you can visit me in Spain. We'll sit in the sun, drink crap lager and talk about good times. How does that sound?'

Danny smiled.

'Right,' Colin said, 'I've got a couple of things to sort out before the medics get here.'

He turned to the tall guy. 'You're Ryan?'

Ryan nodded.

'Come and sit with Danny. I won't be long. And keep putting pressure on that wound.'

'Ryan,' Danny whispered. 'You did good_ today. You're a good_ person. Don't let what happened_ change you back into_ a bad person.' He squeezed his eyes shut and grabbed at his chest.

Colin came back.

'I've had a word with the two that are left and let them know that their boss is dead. I took a photo of them on my phone and told them to keep their mouths shut or I'd find them. I've got your guns,' he said to Ryan, who stared at him like a rabbit in a headlight .

Colin snapped his fingers a couple of times to make sure Ryan was paying attention.

'Listen' he said. 'Tell everyone that Chilli asked you to pop by the unit for a chat. You have no idea what it was about, then Terry and the others turned up and tried to kill you. And you don't know why Danny was there. Don't tell them that you had a gun. Just say someone else killed the men, but you don't know who. Okay?' Ryan nodded.

'I'll meet up with Mike and John and tell them what's happened,' said Colin. He knelt beside Danny and took hold of his hand. 'I have to go mate,' he said quietly. 'I'll come and see you in hospital after they sort you out.'

Danny nodded and whispered, 'Look_ after Ryan.' Colin glanced at Ryan and nodded as he squeezed his mate's hand and walked away.

Danny struggled to speak, but Ryan heard him whisper, 'phone_ pocket.' As Ryan fumbled to find it, Danny said, 'Sue.'

***

Phones weren't allowed at the poker club that Harry attended twice a week, so it was a couple of hours before he was able to listen to Connie's voicemail message. He called her back as he got into his car, and she told him about the Range Rover coming over the bridge into Runcorn. She also said she'd received reports of shots being fired at Arkwright Road on the industrial estate. Police and an ambulance were on their way.

In his head, he pictured the quickest route to get there.

'Hold on a second, sir,' said Connie. Harry heard her talking to someone in the background, then she said, 'Gunfire has also been reported at Delph Lane in Moore.' That was only two or three miles away from the industrial estate. He didn't believe in coincidences. 'I'll head up there,' he said. 'Get an armed response unit to that location as soon as you can.'

An ambulance drove past him as he arrived at the bridge on Delph Lane. A PC informed him that two men named Danny Valik and Ryan Thomson were en-route to the hospital, and two other injured men were waiting for an ambulance. The PC drew his attention to the two bodies on the ground. Harry didn't know one of them but recognised the other as Terry Lynch.

'Have you been through their pockets for something to ID them?'

The PC went to his car and returned with evidence bags that contained wallets, keys, money and phones.

'I'll take those,' said Harry.

***

After stabilising Danny in the back of the ambulance, the paramedics turned their attention to Ryan. They stopped the bleeding from his shoulder and put a drip in his arm, wrapped him in a blanket and told him to sit still. The bullet had gone straight through him, missing bones and arteries. He'd been lucky, they told him. Ryan didn't feel lucky. The image of the bad guy crumpling to the ground was on a continuous loop in his head.

I've just killed someone. He's never going home to his family again. He grabbed one of the cardboard vomit bowls from a tray next to him and disgorged the contents of his stomach. He wiped his mouth and took a deep breath. *It was him or me. I was protecting us. I saved our lives, two for one.* It made perfect sense, but it didn't make it any easier for him. *I'm not the guy who snatched Jackie's handbag anymore? Who the hell am I?*

The medics kept Danny alive and on arrival at the hospital they took him directly to the Intensive Care Unit. Sue, Mike and John arrived a few minutes later. Sue stifled a moan when she saw his ashen face. Avoiding the tubes and wires covering his body, she got as close to him on the bed as she could, wrapped her arms around him and sobbed uncontrollably.

He opened his eyes and his lips trembled when he saw her. She moved closer, and he gently kissed her on the cheek. 'No_ regrets' he whispered.

Fifty-Four

The consultants decided that Danny was far too weak for them to operate on immediately. Surgery was arranged for first thing in the morning in the hope that he would regain some strength during the night. Waiting was a risk, but so was an operation.

Sue, Mike, John and Ryan didn't go home that night. They took turns in getting coffees and snacks as the minutes and hours ticked by. There were moments when Danny seemed to regain some colour, but he still needed the machines for support. At some point in the early hours of Monday morning, Sue nodded off to the hypnotic chime of the heart rate monitor. She woke abruptly when the chime became a single tone.

'Danny?'

Within seconds she was being dragged out of the way by medical staff with defibrillators and needles.

Before they had a chance to open him up and repair the damage, Danny's heart gave out. The post mortem revealed that his life-saving mechanical valve had stopped working. With all the stress and constant pressure over the last few weeks, Danny hadn't taken his medication regularly enough to keep his blood thin. A clot had formed around the valve and eventually jammed it shut. The doctors were amazed that he had lasted as long as he did.

Sue, Mike, John and Ryan were there when the doctors gave up trying to resuscitate him and called time. They stood together in silence for what felt like forever. Ryan had never known such sorrow. He turned towards the door to give the family time alone together, but Sue caught his arm.

'Please stay.' He looked at her tortured, tear-streaked face and then at Mike, who was barely holding himself together. Mike nodded, and Ryan stayed with them – where he belonged.

Fifty-Five

One of Terry's men collected Karen from Runcorn. She arrived home to an empty house. Two hours later, she opened the door to two police officers. They told her that Terry was dead.

She put her hand to her mouth. 'How?' she asked.

'He was shot in the back of the head near a canal bridge in Daresbury. Do you know what he was doing there, Mrs Lynch?'

She took a breath and gathered her wits. 'No, I don't. And before I answer any more questions, I'm going to speak with my solicitor. Okay?'

They took her details and informed her that someone would come and see her the following day for a statement.

She poured herself a gin and tonic, took three large gulps and was ready for a refill. She phoned Emma, who was devastated when she heard about her dad. She insisted she stay the night with her mum and would be there soon. Jason didn't say much. He asked if she was okay and made all the right noises, but he wasn't upset. She couldn't handle speaking to Terry's mum, that could wait until tomorrow.

She dialled a number from memory that wasn't saved in her phone.

A man answered. 'Hello.'

'Your baby brother's dead.'

'How?'

'A bullet to the head.'

'Quick and painless, he wouldn't have felt a thing. Who killed him?'

'I don't know the details, but Danny Valik had something to do with it.'

'Danny Valik!' He began to laugh. 'He came at just the right time for us, didn't he. It couldn't have worked out better if we'd planned it.'

She sighed. 'It would be nice if you were here with me tonight, but Emma's coming over.'

'Give me a call tomorrow when she's gone, and I'll come round. It won't look suspicious that way.'

'Thank you,' she said.

Gary ended the call with a smile on his face. *Say hello to the new boss!*

***

Harry and Steve were in charge of the investigation surrounding the killings at the canal bridge in Daresbury as it became apparent they were all related to Jackie Valik's death. The two men alive at the scene had a convenient case of amnesia and couldn't remember why they were there with Terry Lynch.

A search of the area around the bridge revealed spent ammunition shells that forensics confirmed were from an M16 rifle. Harry surmised there had been another gunman.

After Danny died, the only approachable witness was Ryan Thomson. He'd come out of hospital with one arm in a sling and the other arm still in a cast. Harry and Steve interviewed him a couple of times, but his story was sketchy and lacked detail. There was no mention of anyone with a rifle. They also questioned the police officer in the BMW who had followed the Range Rover. Harry wanted to know why he had parked at the shops instead of staying behind the vehicle he was following.

Forensics bypassed the security on Terry's phone and gave Harry a list of numbers, one of which he recognised. It confirmed his suspicions that there was an informer at the station. Accompanied by another officer, he arrested the suspect and confiscated his personal phone. It contained numerous phone calls to several shady characters, including Terry Lynch and Chilli Edwards.

When questioned, the informer admitted hindering the investigation by any means necessary, including pulling the plug – literally – on the CCTV cameras at the station around the time of the attempted abduction of Danny Valik.

'Why did you do it, Steve?' asked Harry. 'You had a good career and a bright future ahead of you.'

Steve was unapologetic. 'You can't say no to people like that, and the money was good. I got two grand every time I made a phone call. I've almost got enough to buy a new house.'

Harry shook his head. 'Your bank accounts will be frozen, and that money will be taken from you. The legal system doesn't look kindly on rogue police officers. You'll be going to jail for a while, Steve, and when you get out, you'll have nothing. I'll be surprised if you ever get another decent job. No one trusts a bent copper.'

Inspector Latchford could not get any new information out of Ryan about what had happened the night Terry Lynch died. His story remained the same no matter how many times he was questioned. The case went cold, and the police file stated that Ryan was an innocent bystander caught in the crossfire of a gangland war. Someone who miraculously survived being in the wrong place at the wrong time.

***

Ryans statement helped to ensure that the amnesiacs were prosecuted under the Criminal Law Act 1967 for lying to protect offenders from being investigated. Harry expected them to be given a minimum sentence of three years and maybe get out of jail in two.

'Something must have really scared them if they were willing to go to jail,' said Harry.

'Or someone,' said Ryan, immediately regretting it.

'What do you mean?'

'Slip of the tongue,' he said, with a shrug of his shoulders.

***

Jackie and Danny were buried together at the church where they were married. Ryan joined Mike, Sue, John, Ray, Anne and all Danny's friends and family to say their goodbyes. Colin was there, devastated that he hadn't been at the hospital with Danny when he died.

He shook Ryan's hand. 'Danny was a good guy,' he said.

Ryan nodded. 'I know.'

As they were leaving the church, Sue linked arms with Ryan, and they walked together for a while.

'Did you know that Danny asked us to look out for you?' she asked.

He shook his head.

'Danny was a good judge of character, and he saw something in you that reminded him of himself when he was younger. He admired you for the choices you were making in your life but thought you might struggle sometimes, trying to find your place in the world.'

Ryan bowed his head and held tightly to her hand. Sue stopped walking and looked up at him.

'Just remember that we're here for you if you ever need us. You're family now.'

Epilogue

She wasn't going to be another statistic, another victim presented on a TV news item about single mothers being taken advantage of in the rented housing market. She'd been raped and beaten by two men in her home because she couldn't pay the rent, and the police did nothing, even after she named one of her attackers!

'Not enough evidence; the guy has an alibi,' they told her over the phone while she was recovering in hospital.

Life for Louise Borrowman hadn't been an easy ride, but she was a proud, law-abiding citizen who did her best in a challenging world. She had raised her daughter Chloe on her own and had only claimed benefits when she was desperate and there was no alternative. She worked hard and saved what she could for the future, but it was never enough.

The anger and shame she felt when she came out of hospital were hard to bear. The experience haunted her and she struggled to get back to everyday life. Her nightmares were terrifying and she feared that her attackers would return. She needed closure.

After work, she started going to the Clarendon to relax and hopefully drink enough to keep the nightmares away. Sometimes she drank a little too much. When this happened, she would open up to Keith behind the bar, frustrated that she couldn't do anything about the savages who raped her.

When she began to cry into her drink, he knew it was time to phone Chloe to come and take her mum home.

After another night of too much melancholic drinking, she got up the following morning with a banging headache. She made the usual promise to herself that she would stop going to the Clarendon after work, knowing that it would be broken like all the other similar promises she had made.

She noticed the business card on the table as she drank her coffee.

'Chloe? What's this for?'

Chloe came into the kitchen and put the kettle on. 'Keith in the pub handed it to me when I fetched you home last night. He insisted that I give it to you. Don't you remember?'

Louise shook her head and immediately regretted it. 'I don't remember much after my fifth G and T, to be honest, love.'

She looked at the black card with the gold inscription. 'There's no name on it. Just a number. What's that about?'

Chloe shrugged. 'He must have given it to you for a reason.'

Later that day, curiosity got the better of her, and she phoned the number on the card. It rang twice, and a man's voice answered.

'Hello.'

She took a deep breath. 'Hi I was given a card with this number on it, but I don't know why.'

'Who gave it to you?'

'Keith at the Clarendon.'

There was a pause. 'My name's Ryan. How can I help?'

THE END

Printed in Great Britain
by Amazon